'Joey takes on his toughest set of
challenges yet in this heart-rending,
triumphant series finale'
Kirkus Reviews

'Features all of the drama, havoc,
and heart readers have come to
expect, dread, and love'
Booklist

'Joey Pigza stays with you long
after the last page has turned'
Carousel

www.**randomhousechildrens**.co.uk

Jack Gantos was born in the town of Norvelt, Pennsylvania, and has spent time living in Barbados and South Florida. He has written books for readers of all ages. He lives with his wife and daughter in Boston, Massachusetts.

THE KEY THAT SWALLOWED JOEY PIGZA

JACK GANTOS

ILLUSTRATED BY DAVID TAZZYMAN

CORGI YEARLING

THE KEY THAT SWALLOWED JOEY PIGZA
A CORGI YEARLING BOOK 978 0 440 87032 6

Originally published in the USA by Farrar, Straus and Giroux in 2014

First published in Great Britain by Corgi Yearling,
an imprint of Random House Children's Publishers UK
A Penguin Random House Company

Corgi Yearling edition published 2015

1 3 5 7 9 10 8 6 4 2

Penguin Random House is committed to a sustainable future for our business,
our readers and our planet. This book is made from
Forest Stewardship Council® certified paper.

Set in 12/15.25 Century Schoolbook by Falcon Oast Graphic Art Ltd.

Corgi Yearling Books are published by Random House Children's Publishers UK,
61–63 Uxbridge Road, London W5 5SA

www.**randomhousechildrens**.co.uk
www.**totallyrandombooks**.co.uk
www.**randomhouse**.co.uk

Addresses for companies within The Random House Group Limited can be
found at: www.randomhouse.co.uk/offices.htm

THE RANDOM HOUSE GROUP Limited Reg. No. 954009

A CIP catalogue record for this book is available from the British Library.

Printed and bound in Great Britain by CPI Group (UK) Ltd, Croydon CR0 4YY

For Anne and Mabel

For Anna and Michel

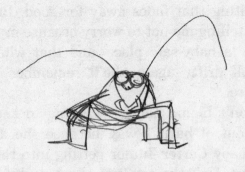

1
HOUSE-OF-PIGZA

I'm Joey Pigza, and here I am again back in my roachy-row house on Plum Street and living my whole wired past, present and future, all at the same time. I'm sure I need a triple med patch for living the hop-skip-and-a-jump life I lead, but at the moment the house seems to have used them all up. A few weeks ago Mom slipped into one of her drifty moods and hid my meds, or maybe she just said she hid what's left of them because we don't have the cash to pay for more. Who knows what she did, because when she's spacy her memory gets all fluffy like skywriting that fades away for good. But she keeps telling me not to worry because my meds are in 'a baby-safe place' and that when she gets all drifty again she'll remember where they are.

I don't blame her for wanting to keep my meds out of harm's way, because she doesn't want baby Carter Junior getting into them by accident. He's the opposite of me, and if he got a hold of my meds I figure he'd get wired up and start zooming around the skirting boards doing wheelies like a psycho baby in nappies, or else he'd be taking a zonked-out snooze for a few months like a bear cub in hibernation. I'm not really sure what my meds would do to him, but either way we'd have to call 911 for an ambulance and the next thing you know the Child Welfare people would haul Mom away for being a dud mom. I don't want that to take place, but my clock is ticking, and without my meds who knows what kind of meltdown I might have in this roached-out house?

In fact, it seems like all the bad things in my life started right here in this crazy house on Plum Street. I even stuck one of my med patches on the front door, but when the meds didn't change our home life for the better, I scrawled *Out of Order* across the patch and left it stuck there. I always thought this house caused trouble, but once we got away from it the trouble just came right along with us like the busted furniture we hauled to the new house. And now that Mom and I and baby Carter Junior are back in the old house with all the old furniture, the bad stuff has started haunting us all over again. Maybe if I lived in a new house, with all new stuff, everything would change for the better. But deep down inside I don't think so. I can't blame who I am on *where* I live, because who I am is *how* I live. My old sped teacher, Special Ed, once told me you really get to know a kid by the type of games he makes up. I think my all-time favourite game was swallowing my house key on a string and pulling it back up with a little drippy lunch dangling on the end, and then doing it again. I perfected it at home, but when I swallowed it at school my teacher cut the string. I won't give you the potty details, but a day later I did get that same key back. It dropped out of my *revolving door* the natural way. And even though I washed it a hundred times with soap and hot water, nobody in class would sniff it – not even if I licked it first!

So, here's my new favourite game. At night, I stand dead still in our pitch-black kitchen and sprinkle a packet of coffee-shop sugar around my feet. Then I take a deep breath and freeze all my muscles as the cockroaches inch out of their hiding places and slowly gather around the sugar for a belly-filling feast. But I wait and wait and wait, and even as I silently stand there with a twisted grin growing tighter across my face, I know this is all wrong. But doing what is wrong in this House-of-Pigza seems so right, so I don't move an inch until my lips are clown-crazy huge and can't stretch any wider without splitting open, and then I flick the light switch and it's *Game on!* The roaches take off and you can hear them chirping with fear as they skitter back to the cracks in the walls. They are fast, but so am I, and my hands slap after them like snapping bullwhips and I flatten a bunch of them. I keep a *Rubbed-Out-Roach* chart written on the inside door of the snack cabinet, which is their private clubhouse. Once I gather up the dead I give myself ten points for the big ones, five for the medium, and half a point for any babies smaller than my fingernail. I figure in a week I'll have a thousand points. I don't have a clue what this game says about me, but after playing it I find myself breathing heavily while hunched in front of the bathroom mirror making Japanese-horror-movie faces as if I'm a terrified little roach and a giant human Joey hand is going to slap the guts out of me.

Or maybe I *do* have a clue about what that game means. Special Ed had also said that everyone in the whole world has a special gift, and my special gift is that I can feel everything everyone else feels. He told me it is the most powerful gift in the world because I can feel everyone's happiness and become super happy, and he also warned me that it is the most distressing gift because I can feel everyone's sadness, and the weight of their sadness can fill me with sorrow and drop me to my knees. I sure know what he means by that because when I hear my mother weeping at night I weep too. It's hard to call weeping a gift, but then again, when she stops crying and laughs out loud I'm never happier.

I'm just trying to get back on track and make sense of myself these days because ever since my parents split up again there is no sense in me hoping things will get better between them. All my life I've had my ups and downs because of their hit-or-miss moments. Each morning they'd roll out of bed like a pair of fuzzy dice tumbling across a game board and I never knew if they would end up even or odd or not. So while I waited for them to bounce off the walls and maybe add up to a lucky day, I'd just stand as still as a pencil drawing of a boy with my eyes X-ed out and my mouth bolted shut as if I was locked out of my own heart and had lost the key.

It's bad to fear your parents, but worse is when you fear yourself. I used to think I was getting better without my meds, but now I feel like I'm returning to the old days when I lived with my grandma. In those days I couldn't look into a mirror without my eyes spinning like carnival lights. Now those old days don't feel so old any more. This morning I looked in the mirror and my eyes were sparking, and right away I had to twist my head to one side and take a deep breath. 'Settle down, Joey,' I whispered. 'Take a time-out.' But my eyes were already flashing: *Danger zone ahead!* I mean, how can seeing me, and being me, be hurting me? How can I be the worst person in my own life? *Please*, if you know the answer, *do get back to me on that!*

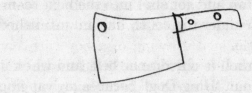

2

MEAT CLEAVER

Dad's still gone. Mom's the boss again, and she said things aren't going to get better now that we've returned to living on the edge. But she orders pizza every night, so how bad can it be? While I wait for the pizza to arrive I dance around the kitchen singing '*O so-le mioooo*' with a pair of white pants stretched around my head like I'm that singing Italian chef on the cover of the Antonio's Pizzeria box. I love how the chef is kind of skipping through the air as he spins a crazy tornado of dough over his head like he's getting ready to serve up a stormy mozzarella with extra lightning and thunder. I tried spinning a dinner plate above my head, but I sneezed and tossed it too high and it hit the ceiling fan and got shot into the next room. It ended up under the couch like an unfinished jigsaw puzzle.

The doorbell is our dinner bell, and when it rings I yell out, 'Ding-Dog!' because my yapping Chihuahuas, Pablo and Pablita, put up more racket than two leaf blowers.

I load one dog on top of the other like stacking plastic chairs, and then hoist them onto my head. They make an excellent hat with their skinny front paws stretched under my jaw like a chinstrap. In case you didn't know this detail about me, I like wearing hats because they keep me from pulling out my hair when I'm jumpy. The Chihuahuas have the *yaps* but I have the *yips* – the kind of crazy yips that baseball players get when they are nervous and can't throw a ball in a straight line no matter how hard they try. My yips are the hair-pulling kind. One moment I'm mindlessly scratching my nose, and then a split second later my hand yips up on a spring and plucks a single hair out of my head as if my fingernails are some kind of evil bird beak. I can't seem to stop attacking

8

myself, so I now wear a Jewish yarmulke to keep me from pecking my own head bald. Mom gave me the yarmulke because after the miracle of Carter Junior being born she said we were going to convert to Judaism and move to the Holy Land and be closer to God. We walked to the library to find out how to be Jewish over the Internet, but it was way too complicated, so the yarmulke and a kosher dairy pizza were as far as we got. Besides, Pennsylvania is always called God's country so I figured we'd just bump into God one of these days and ask for his blessing when he toured through Lancaster.

I love answering the front door because it's always the same friendly Chinese pizza delivery guy, Mr Fong. He's learning English and becoming a citizen and is very nice because he lets me break the welfare rules and pay him in food stamps.

'Pig-zah pie!' Mr Fong announces grandly.

I taught him how to say that.

He bows, and then pulls the pizza out of the red plastic hot box that keeps it warm.

'Thank you for the Pig-zah, Mr Fong,' I say, and smile brightly. He nods, and then reaches out to pet Pablo and Pablita, who lick his hand. They love the taste of him. Mom said to keep an eye on Mr Fong because the Chinese eat dogs, but I have never seen a Pekinese pizza on the menu, just an American pizza with sliced hot dogs and baked beans.

After I glance up and down the street for the welfare police that Mom says spy on us from parked cars, I quickly pay Mr Fong and say, 'Thank you, Mr Fong, see you tomorrow.'

He smiles and his eyes disappear as his mouth opens. 'Thank you,' Mr Fong repeats, and then he tips his flat pizza cap that looks like something you wear when you graduate from Pizzeria College. He's a fast learner.

Then the Chihuahuas and I return to the kitchen. I lean way forward and they spring off my head like kung fu fighters, then stand on their hind legs and chop at the air with their front paws as they bark and beg. I pull a slice out of the box and place it on a chipped cutting board that reminds me of Dad's scarred-up face. I wish he was still around but I don't think Mom does. He called once, and afterwards she dragged herself out of bed and went down to the butcher's shop and bought a used meat cleaver. 'For protection,' she said wickedly, and hid it under her pillow. But later I took it away and re-hid it in the freezer.

Thank goodness I don't have the meat-cleaver yips and hack myself in the head because the cleaver comes in handy for chopping a slice of pizza to bits for Pablo and Pablita. If I don't madly murder it into a thousand crazy pizza slivers, the steamy dough clogs up their tiny throats and they choke, then swell up and fall over, and I have to press down on their puffy bellies with both hands as if I'm strangling a set of bleating bagpipes until the stuck wad of dough shoots out their mouths and *thwacks* against the skirting board. I don't really bother to clean it up, which is one of a hundred reasons why the Humane Society of Roaches sends us all their homeless adoptees. Once I asked Mom what the name 'Pigza' meant and she replied that it translated into 'roach' in Gypsy lingo, so it makes sense that we nourish all our little floor-friends.

Mom is a very fancy pizza gourmet and has me use scissors to cut her slice into long thin strips, which I then serve over lettuce in a bowl with Thousand Island dressing so she can eat it like pizza salad with a fork. She got that foodie recipe from Quips Pub across the street, which serves it for Sunday brunch. The only one in this house who really eats pizza like a normal Pigza is my little baby brother, Carter Pigza Junior, who doesn't have teeth yet but can power-gum an extra-cheesy slice into mush and swallow it bit by bit and wash it down with a bottle of welfare powdered milk, which for some reason is the same mustard colour that comes out of his revolving door two meals later. I love him.

While the dogs and Mom and Carter Junior eat, I use sewing scissors to trim my slices up into little family faces and arrange them on a plate like my own perfect single-size Pig-zah family. With the baby propped up on pillows next to me, I eat my pizza in front of the TV while watching reruns of *Star Trek* because I love Mr Spock. He has no emotions to get in the way of his thinking, which makes him the complete opposite of me, because my emotions always get in the way of my thinking.

After we eat and I clear Mom's bowl from the bedroom there is one perfect slice left over, but I secretly save it for Dad like it's some kind of bait in our rat-trap house. Even though he is still missing in action since he ran off six months ago, I leave the last slice untouched in the box in case he shows up hungry for a midnight snack. He's still slinking around town but he never shows his face at our door, which just means I get to share the last slice with Carter Junior in the morning. I sprinkle a little water on it and stick it in the microwave and give it a thirty-second blast of radiation and it freshens right up, as if Mr Fong had just delivered a breakfast slice at our back door.

I want to share everything with Carter Junior except for my nervous insides. I call him the 'missing link' because so far he's *not* a wired mess like me, because I'm definitely a wired mess just like my missing dad, who needs to be totally rewired because he's a mess like his dead mom, who is also my dead grandma. She's buried in the cemetery behind our house and I can hop over the back fence and visit her. I think she's still wired because when I press my ear flat against her tombstone I can hear the hum of her spinning in her grave like an electric turbine that could brighten up all the dark corners of the world. I wish there was an electrical outlet on her tombstone because then I could plug in a radio and she could talk to me. I'd really like to know what it's like to be dead and lighting up God's private planet but I don't want to die to find out.

As Mom said, I was destined to be amped up. She said I was born so wired I had sparks coming out my ears, but nobody knows about Carter Junior yet because so far he is mystery wired. Mom calls him the 'Perfect-Pigza' and I call him the 'Buddha-Baby' because when I put my ear to his chest it's like listening to a kitten purr.

Still, any way you look at it our family has always been trip-wired for things to go wrong. One step out of line, and who knows what fuse will blow around here, so I try to keep the peace as I eat my family of pizza-people and then let the dogs lick the plate so I don't have to worry about washing the dishes before putting them back.

3
SCHOOL

I have to tell you that I am a little disappointed because after my parents home-schooled me last year I now have to repeat a grade. I guess they used the wrong book to teach me. It was titled *Home-Schooling for Dummies* and it must have worked pretty good because now I feel like one.

'It will be for the best,' Mom had said after I went to where she was camped out in bed and showed her the principal's letter telling me the bad news. 'You'll get a *fresh start*,' she added, and smiled just a little because smiling big takes too much out of her.

'How many fresh starts can you have in life before even *fresh* turns stale?' I replied, and took the letter out of her slack hand before it drifted from her grip and slipped under the bed. She had a way of forgetting she was holding things, which is another reason why I liked holding Carter Junior.

The night before school started I turned the house upside down and inside out looking for where Mom might have hidden my meds, because I wanted to be the best of me when I started school. But I couldn't find them anywhere and I was beginning to feel a little desperate, so I went to her bedroom where she was lying down and gazing up at the ceiling stains.

I leaned over her until we were nose to nose. *'Think!'* I said, staring into her watery eyes like I was dipping into her memory. 'Where are my meds? *Think*,' I repeated, and tap-tap-tapped a finger on the side of her head. 'Hello?'

She suddenly sprang up and pushed me back. *'Think!'* she replied, and in a mocking way tap-tap-tapped me on the head with her fingernail, which was like the needle beak of a woodpecker. 'Have you seen my meat cleaver?'

That conversation went nowhere.

So, on my first day back for a *fresh start* at my old school, I kept reminding myself to be strong, and in control of myself, and to stay on task like Special Ed had told me, because as I walked there I felt a little jangly inside like old Mr Trouble was spying on me through a telescope and snickering while I marched directly towards an invisible trip-wire that would blow up my whole day.

It seems like the last time I was at school I was really, really happy and my meds were keeping me on the straight and narrow, and Mom was energetic, and Dad was out of the picture, but now so much had changed that I was really wishing I had my meds to back me up. I mean, why else was I high-stepping down the sidewalk with my head thrown back and arms pumping up and down like I was the conductor of an All-Star All-Roach marching band while singing one of Dad's old favourites, 'Hey, look me over, lend me your *fearrr* . . .' By the time I strutted up the curved school drive-way I was bug-eyed and sweaty from all my fancy-dancey footwork.

I marched past the row of dusty yellow buses that wanted me to reach out and draw funny faces on them, but instead I jammed my left hand into my pocket. If my hair-pulling yips got the better of me, my left arm would jerk up and down like a demon windshield wiper and I'd pluck my little yarmulke off, and in a flash I'd be half bald. Plus, I could see Mrs Jarzab, my old principal, not too far in front of me, and she was all smartly dressed up in a red suit with foamy ruffles at her neck and sleeves like she was made of whipped cream under her jacket. She was shaking everyone's hand as she sang one of her three cheery greetings that harmonized into one complete song. 'Why, welcome back,' she cried out to the kid on her left, and 'Hope you had a lovely summer,' she chirped like a cardinal bird to the kid on her right, and 'I missed you so much!' she gushed to the next one on her left. I could have used her in my marching band, but instead, as she repeated those three little verses over and over to the kids that streamed by, I held my hands up to the sides of my eyes like blinkers and high-stepped right past her so she wouldn't notice me. But she had a case of the kid-snatching yips, and her arm snapped back and she hooked a finger through my rear belt loop.

'Is that my old friend Joey Pigza?' she asked

warmly, and slowly pulled me back like she was reeling in a dog by its tail.

I turned and beamed at her with my chunky carved-pumpkin smile with the extra orange glow inside, because I was secretly happy to be called an old friend. 'I bet you are pleasantly surprised to have me back again,' I said, and really meant it.

She gave me a hug to hold me still as she stared deep into my eyes and hummed like a little engine picking up speed, shifting through all the many gears of my past behaviour. Finally she backed away and cocked her head to one side like a pirate's parrot as she fixed her gaze on my yarmulke. 'Are you having a good day?' she asked.

'Am I gonna be tested on that?' I replied, because before I left the house my mom did say through her locked bedroom door that I was 'going to be put to the test this year'.

'Remember,' Mrs Jarzab answered as she carefully reached up and removed my yarmulke and tucked it down into my shirt pocket, 'a good day doesn't happen to you, Joey. You happen to *it*.'

Then, before I could think of something clever to say in response, she spun me back round and I lurched forward as she turned towards a kindergartner and sang out, 'Why, welcome back. I missed you so much, and I hope you had a lovely summer.'

I marched through the school's front doors with a smile on my face and wondered what nice thing I could do right away to make my new teacher like me better than anyone else in the class. My favourite teacher, Mrs Maxy, had quit. Everyone said I did her in. One year of having me spinning around in my seat all day while yelling out, 'Can I get back to you on that? Can I get back to you on that?' really tried her patience. But she was strong. She held up for a good long while before I wore her down with a few of my tricks. First, I had a plan to remove my fingerprints and crammed my skinny little finger into a pencil sharpener and gave it a good turn, but only yanked my fingernail to one side like shelling a shrimp. That hurt, but Mrs Maxy didn't panic. She was even OK with me after I swallowed my house key in class and then brought it back for a show-and-tell sniff test. I saw her smile when I said in a Pepé Le Pew French accent that it smelled like 'Pew-de-toilet'. It was only after I went running a little too fast with a sharp pair of do-not-run-with scissors and accidentally cut off Maria Dombrowski's round nose-tip which sprayed blood like a showerhead . . . well, I guess that was just too much for Mrs Maxy or anyone else, and I was taken out of her class and sent to special-ed school. For Mrs Maxy, that short time with me was like a whole fifty-year career.

I bet if I asked her why she quit she would look at me and scratch her chin like she was giving the question a lot of thought, and then she would suddenly holler out, *'Can I get back to you on that?'* She probably has my school picture – the one with my bandaged finger – on her bedside table to remind her that if she even *dreams* of getting another job she should take on something easy like wrestling alligators or being a crash-test dummy.

I liked her, and those were fun times to think about as I walked down the main hall. I looked at my reflection in the glass trophy case and put my yarmulke back on. Then before I found my new classroom I passed the Health Office. My old school nurse, Mrs Holyfield, who always took care of me, had her door wide open. I poked my head round the corner of her door-jamb and yelled out, 'Guess what? Joey Pigza is back!'

She dropped her pen and popped up from her old desk chair like she had just sat on a splinter. 'Joey!' she cried. 'Get your sweet self over here and give me a death-grip hug!' She swung her soft tan arms out wide and gave me a love target as big as her heart. I grinned my impish grin – the one I save for best friends – and lined her up in my sights.

Since there was a desk between us I just took a few steps back, and then revved up. 'Incoming!' I shouted, and launched myself headfirst over her desk like a missile. She didn't have time to duck, and we slammed back against her wall so hard the display shelf of bad dental hygiene came unhinged. Rotten teeth scattered across the hard yellow floor as if they had been knocked out of my own jaw. I counted up the cavities like I do when I open my mouth real wide in the mirror. The black spots in my teeth look like sea urchins hiding in the cracks of coral. I like to gaze past them and dive deep down my throat as if it's a secret tunnel leading to a trap door where I can crawl out and escape myself, and later come strolling back home like a totally normal kid, as shiny and fresh as Lincoln rolling in on a new penny.

But when I give it some thought I don't

really want to be a totally normal kid. It is so much easier to be in trouble all the time because then everyone wants to help you, which makes the other kids jealous: when you are normal it is never your turn to get help, because somebody like me is always at the front of the line like a circus seal bouncing a ball on its nose and slapping its flippers while arfing out 'Me! Me! Me!'

'Joey,' Mrs Holyfield suddenly said, locking my face in front of hers. 'Look into my eyes.'

I did.

She didn't blink. 'You still got meds?' she asked.

'Yeah,' I said breathlessly. 'I got a med patch.' I wished she hadn't asked because when I left for school I swiped the old Out of Order patch off my front door.

'Let's see it,' she said.

I nervously struggled to pull up my shirt-sleeve, and when I did I showed her where I had that old patch rubber-banded onto my fore-arm. It looked a little crusty.

'*Out of order?*' she read out loud, and raised an eyebrow. Then she hunched forward and sniffed at it like a police dog. Her nose crinkled up. 'Pee-yew! When's the last time you changed that nasty thing?' She grimaced, like she was talking about one of Carter Junior's prize-winning nappies.

I started to count days, going backwards from when Mom hid them, but abruptly stopped the instant Mrs Holyfield yanked my old patch off in one painful rubber-band snapping rip and flipped it towards the trash can. Then she spun round and opened the bottom drawer of her filing cabinet. She fingered through a rack of manila folders until she found mine and pulled it up.

'I was hoping you'd return,' she said, and opened my file. 'I hate it when the great kids move on.'

'Me too,' I said. 'Believe me, it feels a lot better to return to a place you love than to leave a place you love.'

'I still have a few emergency med patches left over from before,' she continued as she plucked one out of the folder and ripped the paper wrapper down the side. 'Now stick out your arm.'

I did. She peeled off the non-stick back and slapped it on.

'Thanks,' I said, and then I took a deep breath and leaned way into her like an exclamation point at rest.

After a minute she lifted my chin with a finger and gave me a no-nonsense tell-the-truth look. 'How's your mom?' she asked.

That was a trick question. Once, when I felt bad, Mrs Holyfield said there was a silver lining to me having parents who were a mess because when I'm a mess everyone blames it on the parents. But how I am isn't all Mom's fault.

'She's pretty great, sort of,' I said, and dropped down onto all fours to pick up the jagged teeth. I wanted to sneak a few into my pocket. 'She had a baby, which means I have a brother and he looks just like *me*.' I stressed the *me* part because I was so proud. 'His name is Carter Junior – named after my dad, who is now renamed Carter Senior, or "Mr Adios", as my mom calls him.'

'What's your dad up to these days?' she asked casually, but I knew her methods. Her nice questions were really like magnets attempting to extract secret thoughts out of my brain.

So I pulled my face way back into my neck, and then pulled my neck way down into my shoulders like a tortoise. 'Oh, he's really great,' I said in a choked-off voice. 'He's turned into a new man.' That part about him being new was true because he had gone through a full-on face-lift that got rotten from an infection. He may have turned himself into something like Frankenstein's monster, but I don't know for sure because before he took his bandages off and revealed his new Hollywood Horror face to everyone he ran away from Mom and me and Carter Junior, and all I ever found of him in the hospital parking lot was the scabby gauze bandage that had been wrapped around his oozing face like an infected flag from a nation of zombies.

'Yeah, Dad is lookin' good,' I repeated, thinking it would be best to not say another word – which for me is hard to do.

'I'd like to meet up with him someday,' she replied.

So would I, I thought, but my mouth said, 'I'm sure you will. He'll come in for Parents' Day this year.' The moment I said that I knew it was time for me to go to class before I said more stupid things, like 'Why don't you come over for a big Pig-zah family dinner?'

I took a step towards the door, but she wasn't finished with me and clamped a hand on my shoulder. That's the one thing about always being in trouble. Even when you stop being in trouble, people continue to want to help you because they are never quite sure you have straightened up. I guess once a nail is bent there is no way to make it perfectly straight again. You can *almost* straighten it out, *almost* make it new, but that little weak spot always remains.

'Don't worry about the meds,' I said. 'I'll do some spring cleaning and find them in a sock or somewhere.'

'Don't wait until spring,' she advised, 'because you're already a bit *springy*. You hear me?'

I gave her my big smile again.

She gave me a *pat-pat* on the top of my head like a hammer going *tap-tap* on the head of a nail. Then she lifted my yarmulke and slowly combed her fingers through my hair, where I'm sure she felt around for my old weak spot.

4

THE ORACLE

Like I said, when I'm just a little bit of trouble people give me extra help because they think they can teach me how to help myself, which is always their hope, and mine too. All morning my new teacher, Mrs Fabian, had us studying ancient Greek mythology by acting it out.

'This year we'll live like the Greeks!' she declared with enthusiasm, and pointed to a map of Greece and a list of names and places she had tacked to the wall. She pointed out Mount Olympus, where all the gods and goddesses lived, and the dark underworld called Hades, and told us great stories about the Minotaur and Hercules and so much more ancient life. 'We'll eat, drink and sleep Greek culture and mythology!'

I liked her right away because she was talking about having fun *before* we went over the list of class rules. Still, there was something bothering me that I needed to ask her, so I raised my hand.

'Yes, Joey?' she asked.

'Are we going to be tested on that?'

'Not yet,' she replied, and smiled widely. 'We're going to enjoy learning it first.'

'After we enjoy it,' I asked, 'then will we be tested?'

'We'll see,' she said.

'See a test?' I shot back.

'You are a clever boy,' she replied, trying to put the brakes on me. 'Don't stress out. Always remember that the more fun you have, the better you'll do on a test.'

'But all my life I've been tested and I do stress out a little bit,' I said with my heart pounding inside my chest like a fist punching its way out. 'Because right now I'm repeating a whole year, which means I totally failed *everything* in last year's test. You name it and I flunked it!'

By then I had everyone's attention so I tried to be helpful and blurted, 'Testing turns me into a stress-mess. Everyone else, too!'

'Well, in that case,' Mrs Fabian swiftly cut in, 'you need a fun job that can bring out the best-mess in you.' She snapped her fingers and right then and there gave me the job in class every-one else wanted. I became the Greek Oracle at Delphi and wore a Greek toga around my shoulders as I sat at her desk, and everyone lined up in front of me like troubled ancient Greeks with big problems. Instead of *me* being worried, it was their job to look worried, and then one by one they were to whisper their questions in my ear. My job was to listen, then 'Greekishly' slap my palm up against my fore-head, and roll my eyes inward, and moan like a ghostly wind, and then come up with a prediction. I liked this job because everyone always said I was a natural at being dramatic.

My first anguished Greek was Chuck Darts. 'O Oracle,' he chanted in a wavering voice that Mrs Fabian had first acted out. 'What do you see in my future?'

He didn't give me much to work with, plus

he was my first troubled Greek and I hadn't practised my oracling yet. I have always been better at asking questions than at giving answers, so I hesitated as I twisted up my face into a question mark and scratched the side of my peanut head like a thinking monkey. Then suddenly I flicked my eyes open, and in a whispery voice I told Chuck I had a vision of him on an ambulance stretcher after school. 'You will stick your left hand into a baseball glove . . . and a black widow spider will bite you . . . and your hand will swell up so big, not even Hercules could pull the glove off,' I added dramatically.

'Do I survive?' he asked, with his voice fading away like someone falling off a cliff. He gaped at his hand in horror.

'Watch the TV news tonight,' I replied in my moaning, windy voice. 'If you are not dead, then the Greek gods have spared you.'

I thought I did well, but he must have run off crying to Mrs Fabian because she soon snuck up on me from behind and dropped her arms crossways over my chest like a seatbelt, and then she tightened them.

'Remember,' she said softly into my ear, 'your job is to make sure everyone has a *good* day.'

She lifted her arms and I took a breath.

'Well,' I said, looking straight up at her, 'when am I going to have a good day?' It wasn't that I was having a bad day, but if I had a chance to talk to a real oracle I'd want some answers about my missing meds, and how Mom was going to take care of Carter Junior and the dogs while I was at school.

'Well?' I repeated.

'Not every question gets an answer,' Mrs Fabian replied as if she was the boss oracle.

'Why?' I asked. 'What goes *up* must come *down*, so it figures that every question has an answer.'

'Not in this case,' she explained. 'Some questions go up, up and away – *poof!*' She snapped her fingers above my head.

'That sounds so negative,' I remarked, trying to stay a step ahead of her.

'It's negative to waste your time thinking up questions that don't have answers yet. Relax,' she advised.

I knew she was right, because my brain was built as upside down as an iceberg. All my millions of questions were gathered on the bottom of my brain and I only had a few sweaty little answers melting across the top.

'But,' she said cheerfully, steering right around my negative thoughts, 'when you are *positive*, then every day is a good day. Now, can I make a prediction just for you?' Mrs Fabian asked.

'Go ahead,' I said. 'Peek into my future – but watch out you don't get poked in the eye.'

She held one hand over her eyes and rubbed her forehead. Then she leaned down and calmly said, 'The key for you to have a sunny day is when you unlock all the good in the world, and not all the bad.'

'Is there a keyhole I can peek into and see all that good stuff that's waiting for me?' I asked. 'I don't want to unlock any more bad stuff.'

'Just be positive,' she instructed, 'and even the bad stuff will turn into good stuff.' Then she glanced up at the clock because someone had to go down to the cafeteria and get the classroom snack.

'Pos-i-tive,' I said, cutting the word into slices like a pizza.

'Now say it with the appropriate feeling,' she said, and encouraged me to brighten up my tone by making a face as perky as a sunflower.

'*Pawz-i-tive*,' I said softly, like I was gently petting Carter Junior's head. '*Pawz-i-tive*,' I repeated, until after a few tries I made that word sound like it had an optimistic future. 'I'm *pawzzz-i-tive*,' I said to Mrs Fabian, and licked my lips because all those 'zzz's tickled them.

'And I'm *positive* you are,' she replied. 'Now be a ray of sunshine. Remember, your good-day reward will be waiting for you once you make everyone feel less *negative*.'

Secretly I knew she really stressed the word *positive* because of my past, and even though she didn't know a whole lot about my present, I could tell that someone had filled her in on me before I even walked through her door. I bet she had a file on me titled JOEY PIGZA: *TOP SECRET!*

I told the next kid there was a dollar in lost change behind his couch cushions. That was positive.

'O Great Oracle,' a girl named Shirley asked, bowing towards me as she spoke, 'what will my mother cook for dinner?'

'What's your favourite food?' I moaned.

'Chicken under a brick,' she replied.

'That's exactly what she is cooking,' I said, sounding a little astonished. In a million years I couldn't have guessed that people would eat a poor chicken after they flattened it with a brick.

The next kid was missing his tortoise and I said he'd find it in his bedroom slipper – his left one. Another kid wanted to know what was for her birthday. I told her the answer would show up in her wildest dreams just before her alarm clock went off.

By the time I finished with the whole class I was pretty good at being positive. The other kids even smiled at me as if I had been handing out candy. As a result I sat up smartly in my seat and tilted my head back. I closed my eyes. Now it was my turn to ask the Greek gods a question and receive my own special answer. I took a deep breath. 'When will my mother feel better?' I dared to ask.

At that moment a stuttering, scratchy intercom voice came on over the classroom loudspeaker.

'Mrs Fabian,' the sandpaper voice said. 'Can you hear me?'

'Yes,' Mrs Fabian replied loudly, glancing up at the speaker. So we all glanced up at the speaker, which at that moment looked like a round-faced oracle from Mount Olympus about to tell us something important.

As we waited for the office voice to return we heard some switches clicking back and forth, and then a worried, desperate voice came snaking through the speaker. 'Only Joey can help me,' the voice said in a whispery way. 'Only Joey.'

Everyone in class suddenly turned and looked at me. 'Who was that?' asked a wide-eyed kid.

'A Greek goddess?' someone guessed.

But it wasn't a god or goddess. It was my mother. But how could it be her? I must have been hearing voices. I shot a puzzled look at Mrs Fabian, and she was staring right back at me.

Then the switches clicked back the other way and the secretary's voice returned. 'Sorry about that,' she said breathlessly, and quickly added, 'Send Joey Pigza down to the office – *immediately!*' I knew it! Someone must have asked that radio oracle to name the first kid to get in trouble on the first day of school.

But why would the Oracle sound like my mother?

Mrs Fabian turned her eyes towards the door. Her nose was like a needle on a compass and I slowly sailed away. 'Are they going to test me on something I know?' I asked over my shoulder, hoping they would test me on changing nappies and cleaning up baby puke because I'd done a lot of that this last while.

'I think they are just going to fill you in on something you don't yet know,' she said. 'Don't worry. Skip on down there with your sunflower face held high. I predict it will be good news.'

I didn't have to be an oracle to know it wasn't good news, and the only thing that skipped down the hall was my heart skipping a beat.

5

OFFICE

The office secretary sat at a desk behind the long yellow counter lined with visitor stickers, late sheets, hand sanitizer and a box of tissues. She passed me the phone with her damp hand held over the mouthpiece. 'I've been talking to her for a while,' she said nervously. 'But I think she'll settle down.'

It *was* my mother.

'It's me,' I said into the phone, hoping Mom might say something like *I found your meds! Come home and I'll fix you right up*. But that was just wishful thinking.

'Joey,' she whispered spookily as if there was a serial killer climbing through her window.

'Yes?' I whispered back.

'Joey,' she repeated.

'Yes?'

'Joey?'

'Yes?'

'Joey?'

'Yes! It's me!' I shouted in frustration, and then told myself to calm down. This is how she had been since Carter Junior was born. She repeated everything over and over until all the rubber bands in my head snapped at once. 'Yes?' I said again, trying to sound concerned because if I got mouthy she'd say 'Never mind' and not talk to me for the rest of the day.

The secretary looked up from her desk and raised an eyebrow. 'Is everything OK with the baby?' she asked.

Who knows what Mom had told her? She could say anything when she's in one of her *moods*. 'He's fine,' I mouthed, and smiled.

'Joey?' Mom asked.

'Yes,' I replied.

'Is that you?'

I wanted to snap back and say, 'No. It's Pablo the Chihuahua, Joey's answering service.' I said that once and she started to cry so I didn't dare say it again.

'Joey, you have to come home and rescue me,' she said with her thin voice trailing off into vapour.

'Speak up,' I replied.

'I'm afraid I'm going to hurt him,' she said.

I cupped my hand around the mouthpiece of the phone. 'If it's a serial killer, *please* do hurt him,' I advised. 'The meat cleaver is in the freezer.'

The secretary pushed a thick plank of brown hair behind her ears so she could hear better.

'Carter Junior is not a serial killer,' Mom said. 'He's a perfect baby angel, but I'm exhausted and at my wits' end. I'm afraid I'm going to hurt him. I'm just calling to let you know that I'm walking to the hospital to check myself in. I need a little break, and a nurse I know told me they have a programme to take care of depressed moms.'

'What nurse?' I blurted out.

'I used to cut her hair,' she said. 'She's been helpful, so you have to come home before he wakes up, because the Department of Child Welfare will take him away if they find him stranded again.'

Once, she had left him asleep with the dogs on our front porch and run to Quips Pub on the corner for 'one quick drinkie', because she could look out the pub window and keep an eye on him. But when he woke he somehow wiggled out of his doughnut doggy bed and rolled down the front porch stairs, where neighbours found him on the sidewalk protected by my ninja Chihuahuas. The neighbours threatened to call the cops but didn't.

'Can't you wait until school lets out?' I asked Mom. 'This *is* my first day and I'm off to a good start.'

'I was really hoping I wouldn't have to do this,' she said.

Her voice was so drifty I couldn't tell if she was talking to me or looking into a mirror and talking to her sad self.

'Do what?' I asked, trying to get her to speed up.

'Check myself into the hospital for a few days,' she continued. 'I think I need medication now.'

'Well, tell the nurse to double the prescription,' I must have said too loudly, 'because I need some medication too!'

The secretary gave me a regretful look and I

knew what she was thinking – that I was the same out-of-control kid as I had been before. And to make it worse I suddenly got a case of the yips and my hand shot up and flipped my yarmulke over the counter and my fingers started peck-peck-pecking at my head like old typewriter keys typing 'He'll never change' on my scalp.

'Do you want me to speak with her?' the secretary whispered as she gave me a sad-puppy look and pressed my sweaty yarmulke into my hand.

I rolled my eyes up into my head and thought about it. What would the Oracle at Delphi say?

'Yes,' I replied. 'Yes. Keep her on the line for as long as you can. She'll get over this in a minute and I'll be back.' I handed her the phone, and then I ran bug-eyed out the door.

I think I ran screaming down Chestnut Street as I cut through the centre of town with my arms waving over my head like I was a boy on fire. Nobody could see the flames because they were only burning me up on the inside, where some of Mom's crazy words had been smouldering in me like hot coals just waiting for this moment of weakness to flare up.

Last week I had gone down to Goodwill,

where they were handing out free school supplies. When I returned home she called me into her room and told me that she had caught a 'flesh-eating' infection from decaying people while she was waiting in line to renew her food stamps at the Welfare Office. She was worried that she was going to spread the infection to Carter Junior. 'Don't tell him I told you this,' she whispered. 'I don't want him to suffer.'

'What part of your flesh is being eaten?' I asked her, certain that Carter Junior was in no danger.

'The brain,' she replied intensely, and roughly seized her head with her hands as if she was going to twist it off her shoulders like a bottle cap and throw the whole mushy hunk of it out the window. 'Believe me,' she said firmly, 'it's getting worse.'

'Can't the doctors fix it?' I asked, reaching for her hands and squeezing them tightly in mine. 'Like, give you some medicine?'

'I don't think they can fix things that eat you from the inside out,' she replied, sounding overwhelmed and without any sign of fight in her eyes.

'Well, does this mean the flesh-eating disease is going to swallow you up until there is nothing left but your skeleton?' I asked.

She leaned forward and whispered, 'It's worse than that. First, it eats other people's memories of you so that no one even remembers that you were ever alive. Then it eats your soul so that even God forgets about you.'

'I think you are making this up,' I said shakily, thinking now that she was like an insane oracle.

'I think you shouldn't plan on starting school just yet,' she replied. 'You have to stay home and protect Carter Junior from me. I could spread the disease to him and his little head could be hollowed out overnight.'

I quickly glanced at Carter Junior. He looked like a warm loaf of fresh bread all curled up and asleep in his fake-fur doggy bed. He was fine.

'What do you want me to do?' I asked her.

'Just stick around the house,' she replied.

'OK,' I promised, and then she closed her eyes.

'I need to take a nap,' she said feebly, as if they were her last words.

'That's a good idea,' I said. 'Sleep is the best medicine.'

Then she tilted her head back onto her pillow and pulled the covers up to her chin.

'Keep holding my hand until I drop off,' she whispered.

I did, and when she woke up later that evening she didn't mention any of what she had said to me – especially the part about not starting school. I thought maybe the flesh-eating disease had eaten the memory of our conversation. Then, after Mr Fong delivered our Pig-zah pie and I made her favourite pizza salad, she perked up and took a hot shower and did her nails and hair, and then bathed Carter Junior and kissed him all over his head, which had survived just fine. Her moods could go up up up until she was on top of sunny Mount Olympus, or they could go down down down into the black crack of Hades where they got the better of her.

And now, as I ran down Chestnut Street, I didn't know exactly what was wrong with her, but I had a feeling her mood was sinking down down down again to that dark faraway place where I could never reach her hand to pull her out. I figured there was no nap long enough and no shower hot enough that was going to turn her round this time. She wasn't going to pass through this mood. She was going to wedge herself down into it.

I ran until my lungs felt like burned toast, and I still kept running. My yarmulke flew off my head like a puff of smoke but I didn't slow down. I turned left onto Plum Street, and after a few houses I pounded up our front steps. I reached into my pocket for my house key as I stumbled across the porch. I could hear the dogs barking crazily behind the front door. They were begging me to hurry – *Faster! Hurry! Faster!* – as if they saw the meat cleaver flashing in her hand. I saw it in my mind, and I was shaking so badly I had to use two hands to control the key. I stabbed at the lock like I was trying to blind an evil-eyed Greek Cyclops. Finally the key slipped in. I gave it a good turn and then I lowered my shoulder and pushed. When the door swung open it back-smacked the dogs and they yelped sharply as they scrambled madly across the bare living room floor.

'Mom, I'm here!' I shouted up the staircase. 'Are you and Carter Junior OK?'

'I'm not myself,' she cried. I could tell she was weeping.

I wasn't myself either, but I had to help her. Nobody else would, and she was my mom. As I bent over to catch my breath I reached out to pet the dogs.

They retreated and crouched down under a chair and growled at me.

'I'm sorry,' I gasped. 'I am. I'll give you treats later. I promise.'

But that was a lie. We were out of treats and they knew it.

'I'm sorry,' I said as if I were talking to the whole world.

Then I took a colossal breath that was way too big for my lungs and I swelled up inside like a hot-air balloon.

'Hang on, Mom,' I said, rising up onto my tiptoes. 'I'm here for you!'

Then I kind of floated up the stairs.

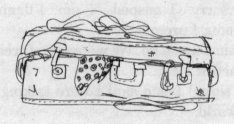

6

RUINED

When I heaved myself into Mom's room she
was half sitting up in bed. The phone was on
the floor and her face was frozen over like she
had hit her own pause button. Whatever button
she had pressed, I wanted to reverse it. Around
her belly button I knew she had that dumb old
tattoo that read *Press here for more options!*
But that was not the button I was looking for.

I stood there panting and swallowing my
own gritty spit until I caught my breath. Carter
Junior was on his doggy bed and playing with
his toes.

'Mom,' I said gently, and touched her shoulder. 'It will get better. Don't give up.' I reached round and massaged her damp neck. I glanced at her bedside clock. The battery was nearly dead and the second hand twitched with less and less effort, like a worn-out heart.

She raised her head and gazed up into my eyes, and as she quietly wept, the tears flowed down her cheeks and pooled inside the closed world within me. Nothing was going to change for the better. Her tears were drowning both of us.

I remembered something else sad she had said to me last week before she started locking her door most of the day. 'If I don't get help soon,' she had said, 'I'll flip out like before. I'll find your dad again and run off and do to Carter Junior what I did to you.'

'No you won't,' I had replied. 'I won't let you.'

'Even if my body is still in this wretched trap of a house, my mind will have run off,' she said.

'That's not true,' I replied. 'Not at all.'

'Look at me.' She sighed and slumped back into her pillows. 'What you see is not what you get. I'm depressed from the neck up. One of these days you'll come home and find me with my head in the oven.'

'Don't say awful things like that,' I had said and gave her a brave look in return, but I was so upset I later walked downstairs and found some old packing tape and taped the oven up.

It had been one sad mood after another since Carter Junior was born, and now all those moods had added up to beat her down. She looked like something that died only you don't know it yet, like a winter branch that gets hollow from the cold and doesn't grow back in the spring, and you just snap it off and throw it over our back fence and into the cemetery. I knew there was still a little life deep inside her and I wished I could stir up a spark and make her furious with me. I wished she would smack me across the room, or say something hateful, or curl her lip at me like a mean dog. But she wouldn't even heat up and give me her anger. She gave me nothing.

I pulled some baby wipes from a plastic tub and gave them to her.

She blew her nose. 'I've been through hell and back, Joey,' she finally said. 'I only have it in me to straighten up one last time. Once and for all I have to fix myself right or I'm done for.'

'You're not done for,' I whispered. 'Stay *pawzzzitive*. Put your best foot forward.'

'If I take just one more baby step forward it will be to jump off the edge of a cliff. Believe me, Joey, I'm not good. I'm broken. I'm beaten down.'

'I'll fix you a cup of tea,' I said, because I didn't know what else to say. 'With honey.'

'I'm leaving,' she said quietly.

'What?' I asked, because her voice was like rustling leaves.

'Leaving,' she repeated with sudden strength. 'Get my suitcase.' She pointed towards her small closet, which was, as she put it, 'a casket for clothes'.

I opened the closet door. The clothes were shoved in any old way as if they had been caught in a stampede. Her battered suitcase was on a top shelf. When I jumped up and pulled it down, an avalanche of scuffed shoes and empty boxes tumbled onto me. I flicked open the snaps on the suitcase and hesitated. I was afraid to open it. Who knew what she might be hiding inside? She looked so crazy I thought she was going to tell me to put Carter Junior in there, but now he was asleep with his ear next to the little radio speaker that broadcast white noise.

'You don't have to do this,' I said to her,

meaning everything – her giving up, and packing, and leaving us.

'I have to,' she replied, and slowly ran her hand over her face as if she were mapping her sadness. 'My hair is a mess. I've let myself go.'

'That doesn't mean you have to leave,' I replied. 'I can fix your hair.'

'I'm sure you can,' she agreed. 'But it's more than hair. It's what's under the hair. I need help in the head.'

'I can always do more,' I offered. 'I can be your houseboy. You can do all the resting and I'll do all the working.' But I knew her mind was made up.

Suddenly she pulled back the bed sheet and surprised me. She was already wearing high heels.

'I'm not running out on you,' she said tiredly. 'It's that I'm sick. Depressed. I honestly don't mind if I hurt myself. It's Carter Junior I worry about.' Her voice was jittery. 'He's still good but I'll ruin him. When he cries do you know what I do?'

I hesitated because I was suddenly thinking about the meat cleaver. Maybe she had got up when I was at school and gone into the freezer and found it, and now she had it in the hand that had slid back under the covers.

I took a slide-step towards the door. 'What?' I said softly.

'Well, I'll tell you. When he cries I pick him up and toss him into the air.'

'He likes that,' I said. 'It's a game. It makes him stop crying.'

'Maybe with you it's a game, but with me I keep thinking if I throw him higher he might hit the ceiling and quieten down. Sometimes I almost let him drop to the floor, and I can see his little eyes pop open and I can tell that I'm filling him with fear. A mother is supposed to give love, but I can't because I hate myself, and now I'm so full up with self-hate I'm filling him with the overflow.'

'But I'm not filled with hate,' I whispered. 'You did OK with me. If you cut me open with the meat cleaver, you'd find nothing but love inside me – the love you put there. Really.'

She wiped her eyes and nose. 'You,' she said, pointing the balled-up tissue at my forehead as if she was pointing at a defect. 'I already ruined you. Inside, your head is a ticking time bomb. One day you'll wake up and do something awful, and you won't mean to do it, but you'll be thinking of your lousy mother, and how I made you crazy, and you'll *explode*.'

'Why are you telling me this?' I shouted, because every day I worked so hard at not going crazy, and now my own mother said I was crazy. I expected my hand to go mental with the yips and pluck out every single hair on my head. My pulse was pounding and my blood was so boiling hot I felt like I was about to erupt through my skin like a human volcano. 'Why are you saying this stuff?' I asked. 'Why?'

'Because I'm sick,' she hissed. 'And I'm going to hurt Carter Junior if I stay, and he is pure goodness and I don't want to do to him what I did to you.'

My shoulders dropped and I could feel something in me break and give up because I knew there was a part of me that was ruined. If you looked at me, I was like a perfect piece of fruit you pull from a beautiful tree, but when you bite into the fruit you find the whole inside is rotten. Maybe she was right. It was too late for me, but not for him. He was still the perfect Pigza and had to be protected.

She stood up and pulled her stretchy shirt down to her hips and stepped towards the open closet. 'I hate these crappy clothes,' she said with sudden fury, then snatched a few things without really thinking about it.

'Don't go,' I said, begging.

'Don't talk,' she replied, and suddenly she hunched forward and gagged as if she was going to throw up, and I wished she would throw up because maybe some of the hate inside her would vomit out and I could clean it up and rinse it away. 'The food stamps are in the drawer,' she said between halting breaths. 'If you run out, call me.'

'Do you need a cab?' I asked.

'I know my way to the hospital,' she replied. 'Over the years I've worn a path down to that emergency room. It's like a church for me.'

'Can we all go together?' I asked. 'Like one big sick family? We could get an apartment there and they could fix me too.' I smiled my big sunflower smile.

She didn't smile. She didn't even answer. Instead she held up a finger to let me know a distant thought was on its way. Suddenly it arrived, and she loudly blurted out, 'Promise me!'

I jumped back. 'Promise what?'

'Promise not to tell anyone I'm not here. I told the school secretary I needed you with me for a few days, because if Child Welfare finds I've left you two alone, they'll take Carter Junior away – and you too. So promise you'll take care of him and not let the state hand him to someone else – some other mom. That would kill me for sure if they gave him to a better mom. Even though it would be good for him, it would kill me.'

'I promise,' I said.

'Prove it,' she insisted.

'Cross my heart,' I added, and slashed an X across my shirt as if it was a treasure map, and below the X was my heart wrapped up in chains, and inside that was my promise not to let anyone hurt us.

She nodded her approval.

'And one more promise,' she said in a deeper voice. 'Don't let that man steal him.'

'What man?' I asked.

She lunged at me and I pulled back, terrified.

'The man who stands across the street at night with a mask on.'

'I've never seen a masked man outside,' I said.

'He's in the shadows,' she whispered harshly. 'I see him. He's shifty, but I know those shifts. Your father is out there – lurking. He wants the baby.'

I glanced towards the window.

'I know I sound a little out of my mind,' she said, reading my thoughts. 'I'm a little too sad, and a little too afraid of myself. It's like your father stole the best parts of me. He took the happy me away and left the sad one behind. He'll steal the good out of you too. And he'll steal Carter Junior because little Junior doesn't know sadness yet. He's not like you and me. Carter Junior is still pure, and that's what your dad wants. Something that isn't spoiled.'

I knew what Mom meant, because I stayed awake at night just wishing I was perfect and happy and smart and that everyone liked me and that when I came home from school my mom and dad were both waiting and when I opened the door they hopped up from their chairs and did a little happy dance around me and sang a cheerful song because I was the sweet centre of their lives. I was the sun and they were my planets, and when they danced around me my face beamed and beamed with happiness. Then they would cook for me and help me with my homework and tuck me into bed. I knew that wishful dream from hoping for it all my life, and suddenly I could feel that my dad had that dream too. In his dream he wanted something that he hadn't screwed up yet. He wanted something unspoiled that would be the new centre of his life – something he could hold in his arms and cook for and tuck into bed. And that something was not me. It was little Carter Junior.

'Promise me,' Mom said, and gently touched my face like she does when I'm sleeping and she is sneakily treating me like a baby. 'Promise me you'll take care of the one pure thing in this house. Just for a few days. A week maybe.'

'But how can I take care of him if I'm ruined like you said?' I asked.

'You were broken once, but you healed and are stronger. You have what I want,' she said. 'Inner strength. Self-love. You have it. I want it. Carter Junior is full of it and your dad wants to steal it. Don't you let him!'

She picked up her suitcase. 'I'm going,' she said.

'Can I visit?' I asked.

'I'll call when I get situated. I'm not sure what they are going to do with me. I don't care, as long as they do something. Now close your eyes and count to a hundred,' she ordered, and pushed me facedown onto the bed as if she was robbing me of herself. 'And keep them closed.'

'OK,' I replied with my voice muffled by the pillow. I listened as she descended the stairs down to the first floor and walked across the living room. The dogs yapped a little after she opened the front door, but since it wasn't Mr Fong with pizza, they grumbled and settled down. Mom carefully closed the door behind her, but I could still hear the sharp snap of the lock and feel a little shudder run through the spine of our house. Then she walked slowly across the porch and down the outside stairs. When her shoe hit the concrete sidewalk I heard the scrape and gouge of the bare metal tip of her high heel, then the other. Then she picked up speed, and *tap-tap-tap-tap-tap*, she hurried away as if someone was chasing after her.

It was easier for me to imagine her as just a pair of scuffed-up shoes that were running away to be fixed at the shoe repairman than to think of her as a mom who had to leave her kids behind in order to be fixed at the hospital.

When I couldn't hear the tapping any longer I opened my eyes. The room seemed especially silent, not just because she was gone, but because my mind wasn't racing from trying to guess what awful thing she might say.

That's when Carter Junior began to cry.

'Hey, perfect buddy,' I called over to him as I hopped up and went to his doggy bed. I picked him up and held him tightly, and he quietened down. 'When am I gonna have a good day?' I asked. He looked up into my face and smiled. Suddenly I could feel my special gift working in a good way, and a smile spread across my face.

'Come on, you bucket of pee,' I said in a silly pirate voice. 'Let's get you a fresh nappy before somebody swabs the deck with you.'

7
BOUNCE

Here we go again. Just when I thought one good parent was better than two lousy ones, I end up with no parents. What kind of family arithmetic is that? But what else could I do? I had to take care of Carter Junior. He was *my* brother and now I was the man of the house – *my* house. And as Special Ed said to me, 'When you have bad thoughts just give your head a good shake and throw 'em out so you can make room for the pawzzz-i-tive thoughts.' When I woke up the next morning I decided that's exactly what I was going to do with the house.

I was going to shake it up, and clean it out, and raise Carter Junior in a house that was fit for a little Pigza prince, and not just a racetrack for roaches!

I figured I'd start from the top down – and that meant getting into my mom's closet. I ran down to the kitchen and grabbed the roll of trash bags and ran back up before Carter Junior could break through the wall of pillows I'd made and flop off Mom's bed. He was always slipping over the edge headfirst like he was going over Niagara Falls.

When I got back upstairs he was fussing so I had to take a time-out and give him some milk and change his nappy. And then I let him play on the floor in a heap of Mom's old clothes while I got busy.

As it turned out, Mom's closet was like a secret bank vault. Once I started going through all her pockets I started finding change and dollar bills and food stamps, and every time I found something good I'd yell out '*Cha-ching!*' and shove it into my pocket, and then if it looked cockroachy I'd throw the old dress or blouse or trousers or shoes into the trash bag.

About ten bags later I finished the closet and dragged the trash across the floor and heaved

62

the bags out her bedroom window and down onto our front yard, which looked like our own Pigza pigpen. Nothing grew there. It was all scratchy brown weeds and hard-packed dirt decorated with orange and white cigarette butts, pancaked beer cans, loser lottery tickets, and flimsy plastic store bags that danced a ghostly litterbug jig each time the breeze kicked up a dance tune.

After all the busywork I got Carter Junior up and dressed and we went down to the grocery store to spend our newfound money. I got two bags of mostly baby food. I got one bag of cleaning supplies and one with nothing but peanut butter and crackers because I knew I could live on that for ever. And when we checked out I tripled the plastic bags just for Carter Junior so I could haul him around by the handles like he was a big old fish flopping around in there. I put him in the shopping trolley with the other bags, and then I made a little train by shoving two more trolleys onto the front. We made a crazy racket as I pushed out of the parking lot, and we went road-racing down the street while steering wildly left then right around the deep holes where they were fixing the gas pipes. Carter Junior liked the wild ride but kept rolling out of his bag and climbing up the side of the trolley to lift himself over the edge. He wasn't in danger because the tops of the other trolleys kept him caged in, and since I was the man of the house I had to spell out the rules of the road to him. 'Rule number one,' I said, raising my finger in the air as we rattled down a hill. 'From now on no Pigza shall harm him- or herself!'

I think that rule calmed him down, and he was a lot happier when we got home and I let him out of his bag. We had a good hug, and then Pablo and Pablita lick-kissed him about a hundred times and I changed his nappy again and washed his hands and face and gave him a bottle. I put him on the couch to watch Spanish soaps on TV. Someday he'll be bilingual, but for now I really wanted him to learn how to make those huge Spanish facial expressions so his face would tell me exactly what he was feeling.

So, while he became bi-facial, I roach-proofed the kitchen cabinets. I didn't want to use any bug spray because of the baby and the dogs, so I just set out the Roach Motels I'd bought, which were creepy because I started imagining what it would be like to spend a deadly night in one. I wish my special gift didn't make me sensitive to the family lives of roaches because, really, I had to kill them.

While I was cleaning the cabinets I got some more trash bags and started throwing out all the old food that had been half eaten by us and rejected by the fussy roaches. We had a lot of dented cans of soup and chilli and tuna that we got for free because when no one was looking Mom would drop the can on the store floor and step on it with her boot and crush in the side. Then she'd ask the lonely-looking manager with the label gun on his sagging plastic belt if we could have it for free, or half price. Usually we got it for free because Mom dressed up special to go food shopping and put on lipstick and perfume and a fluffy pink sweater. Her rule for me in the store was to stay with Carter Junior in a different aisle and act like we didn't know her – until later, when I had to carry home a lot of dented cans and crushed boxes of cereal and expired cottage cheese. I didn't like it when Mom said that for us 'America should be the land of the free *everything* because we were part of the land of dented lives'. I guess that's why we also had a lot of coffee-shop sugar packets, and stacks of paper napkins, and coffee stirrers, and powdered creamer and pats of butter, and toothpicks, and disposable chopsticks, and plastic utensils, and Styrofoam plates, and straws, and a whole drawer full of ketchup packets and mustard and mayonnaise and hot sauce and half-rolls of toilet paper she got at the public library. If it was free, we had it. 'Even kids are free,' she had announced.

And even running away from your kids is free, I thought. *Even losing your mind is free. Getting sick is free. Being alone is free. Being poor is free. Being afraid is free. Being ignored is free. Having crummy parents is free.* I had to stop thinking that way because even torturing myself with sad thoughts was free.

So I kept busy, which is always the best free medicine for me. After checking on the baby, who was sound asleep with both dogs curled up next to him like a pair of furry bedroom slippers, I threw out all the old dented food and free junk, and I put our new food in a clean kitchen cabinet and got some tape and sealed the edges of the cabinet door so the roaches couldn't sneak in. That made me feel better.

Then I opened another cabinet door and taped a piece of paper to the inside of it and drew a week calendar with seven squares.

In square number one I wrote, *Mom left*. In square number two I wrote, *Cleaned house*. Then I looked at the last square. 'O ancient Greek Oracle,' I whispered quietly, in case she was asleep. 'Do I dare write *Mom returns*?'

I closed my eyes and waited for an answer. And then I heard Mom's voice saying, *'Inner strength. Self-love. You have it. I want it.'*

'Thank you, Oracle,' I said, and raised my eyes towards the shiny spot on the ceiling over the stove, because there was a lot of ancient grease up there.

I drew two little humans and two little dogs under the calendar. 'O Oracle,' I said while I had her attention, 'if Mom asks, tell her we'll be here for her no matter what day it is.'

After I did that I felt a lot more hopeful and remembered some good advice Mom gave me. She said the best way to find anything that was lost was to just act like the person who lost it in the first place. Since she was so spacey when she lost my meds, I took a break from kitchen work and ran around the house in circles until I got falling-down dizzy and spacey and then I started looking for my meds. I opened the hall coat closet and went through those pockets and found a handful of change, and then I spun round again until I was good and wobbly, and cracked my nose on the edge of the door as I lurched sideways into the bathroom. I opened the medicine chest. There was some old tooth powder and a rusty single-edged razor blade and toenail clippers. But no meds. I gave it one more chance. I spun round and even moaned, 'O Oracle, *please* tell me where my meds are hidden.' I got an idea and went upstairs into the empty bedroom across the hall from Mom's. There were some boxes of Christmas decorations stored in the closet. I clawed through a few cases of lights and crushed ornaments but found no meds. What totally spacey planet could she have been on when she hid them? I thought.

Then I heard something clatter loudly and go thump from down below. 'Carter Junior,' I hollered, 'hang on!'

I turned and pounded down the stairs. The front door was still locked but Carter Junior wasn't in the living room. He wasn't in the kitchen. I dashed into my bedroom, which was across from the kitchen, just as a baseball slowly rolled along the floor. He was in the back of my closet playing with my old baseball stuff from when I belonged to a Little League team.

'Carter Junior,' I called out, and poked my head under my hanging clothes. 'Hey, buddy, let me teach you how to pitch because I was the best there ever was – until I lost my control and smashed car windows in the parking lot.'

I hoisted him up with my right hand and jammed my left hand into my baseball glove – but something creepy was already in there. For a shocking moment I remembered Chuck Darts at school, and that I had told him a black widow spider was in his baseball glove. What I didn't realize at school was that the prediction wasn't for Chuck, it was for me, and as I wiggled my fingers deeper into the glove I felt the spider bite me. I yelped out loud and flung the glove across the room. Carter Junior saw the bug-eyed fear on my face. He yelped out loud and began to wrestle out of my grip.

When I looked down to see if the spider was coming after us for another bite I saw a bunch of my med patches on the floor and scattered across the room. Ha! There was no spider! Mom had stuffed my med patches into my old base-ball glove! I looked at the tip of my finger and the spider bite was only a paper cut. I began to laugh, and laughed like a maniac because it was the funniest thing that had ever happened to me. The Oracle had worked! It told me exactly where Mom hid my meds.

Then something even funnier happened. I plopped Carter Junior down on my bed, and as I held my stomach and belly-laughed, he held his stomach and belly-laughed. Then when I hopped around, he rolled around. I slapped my thigh, and he slapped his thigh. And when I yelled with joy, he yelled with joy. Everything I did, he did. He was a little me. He had become bi-facial from watching soap operas – or maybe I was his own personal soap opera. He couldn't tell me what he was thinking but he could imitate me perfectly. I sat down on the bed and hugged him and began to laugh. 'I love you, Carter Junior,' I said. 'You are my Oracle helper!' I poked him in the chest and smiled my huge carved-pumpkin smile.

Then he reached out and touched me in the chest and smiled his little carved-pumpkin smile.

It was so great having my own baby brother mirror. And then it was so terrifying because I had to save him from *everything*. I picked up a patch and started to rip open the waxy cover with my teeth, and he picked up a patch and put it in his mouth.

I tugged it away from him, and as I quickly gathered up all the rest of my meds I realized why Mom hid them. She knew he'd want to be like me. She hadn't lost her entire mind. She was still protecting him.

'Thank you, Mom,' I whispered. 'I know you love us. Get better soon.' Then I turned my back on Carter Junior as I quickly changed my patch. 'Come on,' I said to the little copycat, and swooped him up and went into the living room. 'We have to get that trash out of the front yard. Help me load up the trolleys and we'll make a trash train and push this old junk over to Goodwill, and then we have a million other things to do.'

I loved feeling *pawzzz-i-tive*.

8

TAPS

Carter Junior was napping upstairs in his doggy bed and I was still feeling super pawzzz-i-tive. Over the last two days I had finished the laundry, mopped the floors, scrubbed all the walls, washed out the inside of the refrigerator, scraped the creepy crust out of the oven, Ajaxed the stains out of the toilet with the *stinky* brush, and was counting out the rest of the found money and dividing it up into days, when I heard a familiar sound. It was faint at first but then grew louder. *Tap-tap-tap*. It sounded like Mom's shoes. She must have missed us so much she got better right away! And now she was coming home. I didn't have flowers for her, or clean sheets back on the bed, or even a card, but the house was like a present for her, and when she walked up the steps and across the porch and opened the front door she was going to see that every room was spick and span, and that I had quit playing my insane-boy killer roach game, and that all our junk was thrown away, and that I had taken care of Carter Junior, and most of all that I had protected him from Dad. That is what would be inside her present. And as a bonus gift I would show her where she wisely hid my meds and that I was totally on task and ready to perform her every command.

Tap-tap-tap.

She was getting closer. I couldn't stand still. I was so excited I dropped down onto all fours and ran in circles with the dogs just to burn off some extra energy. My chest filled with pride and I could just hear her praising me by saying, 'Joey, you are the *man* of this house.' Suddenly I hopped up and ran to the kitchen just in case a daring roach had snuck out of its motel before checkout time. But they were all still taking an eternal snooze. Then through the open window

I heard something go *thwack-thwack-thwack*. That did not sound like Mom. It sounded like a human weed-whacker or a person with a stick who was slapping at trees and telephone poles and porch steps and garden gnomes and aluminium chairs and parked cars. Then I heard some stranger holler out, 'Ouch! Hey, watch that!' Then a dog yelped and whimpered. Glass broke.

Thwack-thwack-thwack. It was coming my way. Maybe the cure didn't work for Mom and only turned her sad mood into a bad mood, because when she is in a *really* bad mood the whole world can be *dented* up.

But in a moment it was back to *tap-tap-tap* again like she was kicking up happy sparks from her high heels. That made me feel better. Then a moment later her shoes were *tap-tap-tap*–dancing up the front stairs. Any second she was going to tap right into the house and back into our smiley-better lives.

I glanced in the oval hanging mirror by the door and ran my shaking hand through my hair. 'Be a perfect boy,' I said to myself because I knew my in-control perfection would be the best welcome-home gift to her.

Then suddenly it was three window-rattling

*thwack-thwack-thwack*s on the front door.

'Coming, Mom!' I yelled out like a gigantic mouth on wheels. 'Coming!'

I took a deep breath, pulled my shoulders back, unlocked the door and swung it wide open.

'Mom!' I sang out with my sunny-side-up face. I halfway raised my arms for a hug – and then I gasped. It *wasn't* Mom.

It was Olivia, my old girlfriend, and she was the meanest blind girl in the world, and the only girl I had ever kissed. But I didn't want to kiss her just then because I might lose my lips.

She was hissing away like a burning fuse on a scowling bomb – and then she exploded! 'I'm not your mother and I never will be,' she said sharply, then swiftly she raised her long blind-girl stick and *thwack* – she slashed me right across the knee. It could have been a mistake. Or maybe not. It certainly wasn't a love tap. 'Welcome to the House-of-Pigza,' I whimpered, and limped aside.

'Don't talk!' she ordered. 'Just get out of my way – I've been travelling all night.' She raised her stick to strike me and I retreated.

She tapped her way into the middle of the living room, then hovered menacingly while swinging her head to the left and to the right like a storm cloud searching for a place to rain. I dashed round her and closed and bolted the door.

'Why are you wearing a sign around your neck that reads *HELP! Blind Girl Hitchhiking*?' I asked, nervously chattering away. 'Isn't that risky? Why would you wear a black dress to hitchhike at night? Besides—'

'Quiet!' she said bluntly, and stomped her foot. 'I'll tell you more later.'

But I couldn't wait for later. 'I thought you were boarding at that special church school for blind girls your parents sent you to,' I said.

'I've been suspended,' she announced with a sneer.

'That's insane!' I cried out. 'How can a blind girl be suspended?'

'What a stupid thing to say,' she snapped back. 'Blind girls get in trouble too, and you know how much I *love* trouble.'

I knew. We had been home-schooled together by her mom for a while. I still had the scars.

'I'm sorry,' I squeaked. 'What did you do?'

'I refused to go to my anger management therapy,' she said.

'Is that all?' I asked.

'Well, I spray-painted graffiti,' she added with pride.

'What did you paint?' I asked.

'I spray-painted *I AM NOT ANGRY!*' she replied. 'A hundred times all over the school!'

'Did they suspend you for bad blind-girl handwriting?' I asked, and laughed at my own joke.

'Don't make me *angry*,' she ordered, and raised her stick. 'Now just listen. I have an emergency.'

'How can I help?' I asked.

'Do you still love me?' she asked right back.

'Yes,' I said, keeping a sharp eye on her quivering stick, which I noticed was spray-painted tar black and was scarred up from hitting everything that dared to stand in her way. 'The last time you were home, I told you I'd love you for ever.'

'Are you willing to do *anything* for me?' she pressed. '*Anything* at all?' She raised the stick like a trembling conductor about to strike up the band.

I knew her aim was deadly. She could swat flies out of mid-air. Her killer aim was one of the things I loved about her. Except when it was aimed at me. I lifted my arm in self-defence and began to wince in advance of an expected blow.

'Sure,' I said to her. 'I'll do anything.'

'Then I need you to go buy me some underwear,' she said.

'Excuse me?' I replied, and took a hesitant step back.

'*Panties*,' she repeated as if I were deaf, and leaned towards me.

'Why?' I asked. 'Why so suddenly?'

Thwack! She got me right across the shoulder. 'Just listen!' she insisted.

I soundlessly squatted down like a frog on all fours and held my breath. I figured it would take her a few failed slashes before she could target me again.

'Are you trying to look up my dress?' she cried out angrily, and raised the stick so high the tip stabbed the ceiling.

'No,' I croaked. 'No. I wouldn't ever look up a blind girl's dress.'

'But you would look up a sighted girl's dress?' she asked, more as an accusation.

'No,' I quickly replied, and shuffled back across the floor because I feared her anger. 'I don't look up skirts or kilts or anything with an open bottom.'

'Then stand up and talk like a man,' she commanded.

'How did you know I was ducked down?' I asked, slowly standing.

'Blind-girl radar,' she stated with pride. 'Now watch this.'

And before I could watch anything she lunged forward and pressed the sharp tip of the stick right between my eyes.

'OK,' I sort of yelped. 'You win. Let's just talk about underwear.'

'Panties!' she insisted.

'So where are yours?' I asked.

'Say that word,' she insisted.

'Pan-tees,' I said slowly, and squinted cross-eyed at the tip of her stick. 'What happened to your pan-tees?'

'I lost them,' she replied irritably.

'How?' I asked. 'It seems kind of hard to lose something like that.'

'Well, I did,' she said frankly. 'At a gas station bathroom.'

'But how?'

'I rinsed them out in the sink and then I spread them across the hand blower to dry off and pressed the button. The hot air must have heated them up and they floated away like a balloon – I searched everywhere but couldn't find them.'

'What happened to your famous radar?' I asked.

Thwack. Right across the fingers.

'OK, I deserved that one,' I whimpered, and stuck three dented fingers in my mouth.

'Now go get me some panties,' she repeated.

'But I've never done that before,' I replied. 'My mom buys her own panties.'

'Nothing to it,' she said. 'Just walk in and buy them like you buy socks.'

'Please don't hit me,' I said, and cringed. 'But I don't have any pantie-buying money.'

'Here,' she said, and reached into her bag and tossed me her wallet. 'I have plenty of money from gambling at cards.'

'Blind church girls play cards for money?' I asked.

'I might have to kill you,' she threatened.

'OK,' I said. 'But how many panties do you need?'

'Buy a three-pack,' she said. 'For starters.'

'Any colour?' I asked before my brain was working.

Thwack! She hit me again. 'They are all the same colour to me.'

'Ow,' I said sharply. 'That's going to bruise.'

'Ha,' she sort of laughed. 'For you it will turn black and blue, but to me it will be black and black. Ha!' She always had a painful sense of humour.

'But I can't go,' I said. 'We have a baby, and he's sleeping and I can't wake him.'

Then she smiled in surprise and lowered her stick. 'You have a baby?' she asked softly, and suddenly glowed with joy. 'A *real* baby?'

'Yeah. Carter Junior,' I replied proudly. 'He's kind of my kid for the moment while my mom's in the hospital adjusting her mood and my dad's hiding out somewhere in town after a bad face-lift.'

'I *love* babies,' she said, ignoring everything else I'd just said. 'At school I do a lot of baby-sitting for the teachers.'

'Really?' I asked. 'People ask blind girls to babysit?'

'I should slash your eyes out for being so offensive,' she said. 'You sound like my mother, who just wants me to be a blind girl nitwit. But I want to do everything people say I *can't* do because when people say I can't do something I get really *angry*.'

'Did someone ever say blind girls shouldn't hitchhike?' I asked.

'As a matter of fact they did,' she replied, grinning. 'But I showed them.'

'Did someone ever say blind girls can't lose their panties?' I asked, and instantly jumped back, but she just frowned and shook her head.

'Was that a blind girl eye-roll?' I asked.

'Good guess,' she replied. 'But really I'm just being impatient.'

'OK,' I said. 'But for now do you want a pair of my underwear?'

'Don't insult me,' she huffed, and made a stinky face. 'I'm blind. Not sick. I don't wear boys' underwear. Now go. I'm chafing.'

'What's that?'

'You don't want to know,' she said, and made an unpleasant face. 'Besides, I need panties because I'm wearing a dress and it's against the universal girl dress code to wear a dress without coverage.'

I slapped my own forehead. 'Absolutely,' I shouted. 'I should have known that!'

Just then Carter Junior began to cry out.

'Where is he?' she asked.

'Upstairs,' I said. 'I'll get him.'

'No!' she ordered, and wiggled her stick back and forth. 'You go get the panties, and I'll get the baby.'

'Let's all go shopping together,' I suggested. 'Like a little family.'

'I can't be spotted in town,' she said in a half-whisper.

'Did the school call your parents?' I asked, alarmed. 'Or the cops?'

'Probably. But my mom's on a month-long church retreat to the Holy Land and my dad is probably on the road driving his big truck. If the cops do show up here you'll have to lie for me,' she said, and blew me a kiss. 'Now go. I'll take care of the baby. I'm good at it. I even volunteered in a hospital with newborns. I love them and they all *adore* me.'

'They let blind girls take care of newborns?' I cracked.

'You'll die for that,' she threatened. 'That's a promise!'

She started tapping her way up the stairs. Halfway she turned and pointed towards the front door. 'Go,' she commanded. 'Or else you'll never see that baby again.'

My heart swelled. 'You are still the meanest cute blind girl I have ever loved,' I cried out, and threw my arms above my head as if I were throwing her a dozen roses. 'You can stay here as long as you want and help me raise Carter

Junior.' I was suddenly so happy and so full of love I just wanted to thank the whole wide world for my good luck, but she gave me one more cross look and I ran for the door because she could throw that stick like a javelin.

I walked nervously down the sidewalk as fast as I could, with my head rotating back and forth like a jailhouse searchlight. I had the police to watch out for, and maybe Olivia's parents, and my lurking father, and anyone from school. I really had to hurry.

When I entered the discount store a few blocks away I lowered my face and marched straight to a part of the women's section I had avoided because there was always some kind of show-and-tell lady stuff going on that made me uncomfortable.

I walked over to a counter where an assistant had her back to me and was folding T-shirts.

I leaned over the counter. 'Excuse me,' I said in a whisper. 'I need to buy some panties.'

She spun round and I nearly fainted. She looked like Mrs Jarzab, my school principal. But she wasn't. 'What size?' she casually replied.

I had already lost my breath and now I felt

my face turn red. 'I didn't know they came in sizes,' I said, barely squeezing out the words.

'Yes,' she replied matter-of-factly. 'They come in a wide variety of styles and sizes.'

'Well, she's a girl size – a sister size,' I quickly added.

'I already made that assumption,' she said kindly. 'And just so you know, girls come in a variety of sizes. How old is your sister?'

'She's eighteen. An adult girl,' I said, lying.

'Is she a big eighteen, or a medium eighteen, or a small eighteen?' she asked.

'Do you have to ask so many questions?' I replied.

She gave me an exasperated look. 'I believe you are the boy who has suspiciously strolled into the ladies' lingerie section and is asking about *panties*?'

'Sorry,' I said nervously, and quickly glanced around to see if anybody Olivia's size was in the store, but there were just a lot of ladies half dressed in the bra department. I quickly turned away.

The assistant crossed her arms and shifted her weight to one hip. 'Well? What size?' she repeated.

'She's your size,' I blurted out.

'Are you being fresh with me?' she asked, and gave me a stern look as if I was trying to be a wise guy.

'No,' I said. 'I really think you are about the same size. And I'll need a three pack,' I added.

'Any colour?' she asked. 'And plain style or with lace?'

'No lace, and black,' I shot back. 'But colour doesn't really matter.'

'Yes, it does,' the lady insisted.

It didn't, but I didn't explain why. I paid for them and anxiously ran all the way home.

When I unlocked and opened the front door Olivia and Carter Junior were giggling back and forth. She had found his nappies and changed him and got a bottle out of the refrigerator and fed him, and now he was looking up at her face and when she smiled he smiled. When she crinkled her nose and sniffed at him like she was a dog, he crinkled his nose and sniffed at her.

'I taught him how to be bi-facial,' I explained. 'Whatever face you make, he makes. It's kind of like a wordless language.'

'It's called *gestures*,' Olivia said. 'Social cues. We took a course on it in school. They want us to walk around smiling brightly all the time so people think we are deliriously happy about being blind. We're not supposed to look like lost cows on a foggy field.'

I smiled. 'You don't look like a cow,' I said sweetly.

She frowned. 'Just hand over the panties,' she demanded. I gave her the bag and she swatted her way down the hall and into the bathroom.

I took a deep breath and let it out slowly. Carter Junior took a deep breath and let it out slowly. We both hoped I got what she wanted.

About a minute later I heard, 'Joey! Get in here. I'm having a problem and need your help.'

I ran over and stood outside the door. 'All you do is step into them one foot at a time and pull them up,' I instructed. 'Nothing more to it than that.'

'You moron!' she hollered back. 'I know how to put panties on. I just can't seem to keep these up and I need to know why. So get in here.'

'I'll be no help,' I promised. 'Because my eyes will be closed.'

'Fine,' she grumbled. 'Then I'll come out.'

'Nooooo,' I moaned. 'Don't come out.'

She began to pull on the inside doorknob.

I held the knob on my side.

'Let go, you loser,' she demanded. 'Or I swear, when I get out of this bathroom I will beat you until you beg to put on these underwear and run down the street screaming *I'm a girl! I'm a girl!*'

That was a worrisome thought.

I jumped away from the door as she pulled it open.

'Now tell me what I'm doing wrong?' she asked.

I stared at her. It was confusing. The panties were all droopy on the outside of her dress and the waistband was so big that it hung off the hem.

'I'm guessing they are too big,' she said, gathering them up. 'Did you buy panties or a slip, because this is kind of like a slip.'

'I think they are too big,' I guessed, and looked away.

'Then you have to take them back,' she ordered.

At that moment I would've rather sewn her new underwear myself. 'Isn't there a rule that you can't return used underwear?'

'Then get me a new pack,' she said impatiently.

'OK,' I said. 'But take care of Carter Junior, and if any strange men come to the door don't let them in unless they speak Chinese, and then it's Mr Fong, the *Pig-zah* delivery man, who is the nicest man in town.'

'Don't fret,' she said coldly. 'I'd slash into bite-sized pieces anyone who would harm the baby.'

'One more thing,' I asked. 'What size panties do you wear?'

'A girl's medium,' she said.

'Got it,' I sang out. 'I'll be right back.'

Once again I nervously scampered down to the store. When I entered the lingerie department the same assistant was still there.

'Hi,' I said, sort of out of breath. 'I made a mistake,' I panted. 'My sister is a girl's medium.'

'Is she really your sister?' she asked with her hands on her hips. 'Really?'

'Nah,' I said right back, and gave her my big grin and planted my hands on *my* hips. 'She's my blind girlfriend – the love of my life! She's the sunshine that brightens the hundred million smiley faces on my Pigza planet!' Then

I grinned so she could see all my teeth but the missing few.

She frowned at me and then stiffly marched over to a case of panties and picked out the correct size. I paid with a pocketful of change for the cheap pink ones, and ran home.

This time the panties fitted, and Olivia was smiling and smoothing down her dress when she came out of the bathroom. 'You passed the test,' she said warmly, and took a calming breath.

'What test?' I asked.

'The mature-boy test,' she replied, and gave me a little hug, and we awkwardly bonked our foreheads together but I didn't mind.

'You could actually say the word *panties* and go buy some at a store without falling apart,' she said. 'Most boys are so *immature*. Most of them would drop dead at the thought of it and that would make me really *angry*.'

'I am the *mature* man of the house,' I replied proudly, with a little swagger in my fake manly voice, as if I bought girl-panties every day of the week. Nothing to it. Piece of cake. Then I glanced down at Carter Junior. He was staring directly up at me and he looked kind of worried, kind of nervous. *He's showing what I'm* really *feeling*, I thought – *only he's not faking it.*

Suddenly the doorbell rang and the dogs started yapping.

'Ding-dog!' I shouted. 'I'll get it.'

'Don't!' Olivia shouted. 'It might be for me.'

'It's just Mr Fong,' I said. 'Don't worry.'

I hoisted Pablo and Pablita onto my head, grabbed Carter Junior, and opened the door. It was Mr Fong, right on time.

'Pig-zah pie!' he shouted merrily, and pulled it out of the hot box.

'Thank you,' I said, and grinned.

I set Carter Junior down on the porch between my legs, and then reached into my pocket for the food stamps. Just when I slipped them into his hand I thought I saw a shadow lurking behind a car across the street. But it was probably Pablo's paws hanging in front of my eyes.

After dinner, when it was dark, we went for a family stroll. I put Carter Junior in the shopping trolley and Olivia and I walked off our pizza bellies. Every now and again, I'd look over my shoulder but I didn't see anyone following us.

9

BLACK BOX

The next morning I was heating up Dad's uneaten slice of pizza in the microwave for Carter Junior's breakfast. I had strapped the baby in his high chair and kept him quiet with a cup of juice. He had woken me up early from his padded playpen next to my bed. Olivia had moved into Mom's room upstairs.

'How's my special gift today?' I said to him, and smiled my big carved-pumpkin smile. He smiled right back, and I felt that smile fill me up with orange jack-o'-lantern happiness. I knew it was going to be a great day when

I could feel what Carter Junior was feeling because he was pure goodness.

Then I looked out the back window and spotted Olivia standing perfectly still in a small circle of freshly kicked up dirt in our messy back yard. She must have got up before sunrise when it was pitch black, but darkness didn't mean any particular time of day for her. And she must also have been very quiet because the dogs hadn't barked when she opened the rear door.

One thing about being with Olivia is that I could stare intently at her from a distance and she would never know it. *What is she up to?* I wondered. Her feet were sprinkled with loose dirt and dead grass, so she had probably knelt down and covered them before jabbing her stick into the ground and standing to strike a mystifying pose. Her body was kind of a tree trunk in a dress with her two arms spread out like branches bent upwards at the elbows. Her fingers were stretched wide apart like naked twigs reaching for leaves that had just blown away. Her long braids of hair were roped and pinned into circles on top of her head and formed a little basket, or a doughnut-thing.

I wasn't exactly sure what she was doing, but

guessing what people are up to is a game that's usually a lot more fun than actually *knowing* what they are up to. Maybe Olivia was Artemis, the Greek goddess of hunting, I thought. Mrs Fabian had showed us pictures of her in the forest with a bow and arrow. Or better yet, maybe Olivia was someone who had just looked into the deadly eyes of Medusa and was doomed by her freezing gaze.

Before I could think of more good Greek ideas Carter Junior started rocking his high chair back and forth like a kidnapped person trying to escape. The buzzer had gone off on the microwave and I was slow to give him his slice of pizza. In less than a minute he had walked his chair halfway across the kitchen floor as he headed for a face-first smash into the counter. I grabbed the chair, unclipped his seat belt, and hauled him outside along with his blanket and warm slice.

'Hey, Olivia. Do you want me to tell you what I think you are doing?' I asked.

'Nope,' she shot back as if she'd been expecting me, and held her pose.

'Then you tell me,' I asked. '*Pleazzz!*'

'I'm the Statue of Liberty for blind girls,' she replied proudly, and jutted her chin out as she straightened up her posture. 'Blind girls should be as free as the birds, and to prove it I'm going to stand here until a bird starts building a nest in my hair.'

'Oh, I thought that was a doughnut-thingy made out of hair,' I remarked.

'Don't be an idiot,' she scoffed.

'I'm not entirely,' I said, grinning impishly and running circles around her. 'I'm smart enough to know that birds don't build nests in the autumn. So you might be out here for a long, long time.'

'It doesn't matter how long it takes,' she said with determination, and puffed out her chest. 'I always have months and months of thoughts to think about. You have to remember that blind girls are daring explorers of the infinite dark world inside the universe of their minds.'

'So what are you exploring?' I asked, and blurted out a goofy guess. 'Like, are you mapping the dark side of the moon?' I flinched once I said that because I deserved a swat from her blind-girl stick.

'Well, to be perfectly honest,' she replied in a voice that was unusually hesitant, 'in a way you could say I'm *always* mapping the dark side of the moon. I wish I was exploring the bright side and could see the man in the moon and climb up his nose and crawl out of his eyes and holler into his ears. But I'm stuck on the dark side, which is all black except for one mesmerizing object which is my nemesis.'

'Why?' I asked. 'Can't you find it in the dark?'

She smiled a little at that stupid joke. 'Oh, I can find it,' she replied. 'Since I was a little kid I've been staring at what I call the black box. From the moment I saw it floating squarely in the middle of my mind it's been my dream to open it and map what's inside.'

'Why don't you?' I asked.

'All my life I've tried, but it's more like a black vault,' she said with frustration. 'Or everything I can't see compressed into a solid tomb of blackness.' She grimaced, then bit by bit lowered the angle of her arms to give them a rest.

Carter Junior was busy gumming his pizza, which smelled cheesy-good and made me hungry. 'Did you get some breakfast?' I asked her. 'I have some peanut-butter snacks inside.'

'Don't leave,' she replied. 'Talking out loud gives sound to my thoughts, and that really helps me think.'

'OK,' I agreed happily. 'So tell me more about what's in your head, because you can't see me and I can't see what you see.'

'I'll try to explain it,' she said, and slowly stretched her neck and rolled her shoulders. 'But it's hard, and really frustrating, because what I'm going to tell you is what I wake up to every day, and go to sleep with every night.'

She made a loose cage with the fingers of one hand, as though what she was about to describe was trapped in her palm. 'Within my mind is a black space,' she started, 'blacker than blindness really – as black as a black diamond at the centre of the earth, or it could be like a black glass of water poured into the black ocean. It could be an endless black echo folding into itself like a shadow inside a shadow. I can describe blackness a thousand ways, but within all that velvety darkness of my blind mind is that gleaming black box. It's right before my eyes – teasing me. All I want to do is open the box, but I can't. I can't break into it, and so what's in it can never break out.'

'So what do you think is in it?' I asked.

She smiled. 'I've mapped that question backwards and forwards,' she said, 'and I truly believe inside that box are trapped all my hopes and dreams.' She paused and propped her hands on her hips and looked off into the distance. I could tell she was staring at the black box as if she was staring into the black eyes of the snorting Minotaur. Then she stomped her foot on the ground and cried out, 'I wish I could just take my stick and smash that box!'

'But you are *my* hopes and dreams,' I said. 'Right here in front of me.'

'That's nice of you to say,' she replied, 'but I need my hopes and dreams inside of me. And as time goes on I fear my frustrations and anger will just set that box on fire. I can already imagine the flames as black as black knives with hot black points leaping up and down. Some days I feel them and they feel like bad dogs clawing at my legs. Those raging springs of fire will turn everything I hope for into a box of black ashes.'

'That sounds pretty awful,' I said.

'And it's ruining my life,' she said fiercely. 'But I can't even find the front or the back of the box, or the top or the bottom. What I do know is it's as smooth and seamless as a solid cube of glass.'

She turned towards me and set her moody

face into a dark scowl as if her jaw was a black box full of angry words. But I could see right into her and I could close my eyes and feel the weight of that black box pressing the hope out of Olivia. I felt her sadness, but I could feel her courage too. Her dark scowl was more like a black bar of soap, I thought, and the more she talked about her anger the more she wore it down and washed it away. I could *feel* that to be true.

'I think you'll be fine,' I said. 'Just be pawzzz-i-tive.'

She frowned. 'That's not likely to make anything better for me.'

'Being pawzzz-i-tive never made anything worse,' I countered, and then I gave her my bug-eyed pawzzz-i-tive look that always made Carter Junior laugh.

'The only thing that is going to make me better,' she continued, 'is to get my hands on that black box. You would think I could because it just floats there – hovering over me like a massive weight that defies gravity. I reach for it but I can never quite touch it, and yet it seems to box me around. When I feel hopeful I think that someday gravity will slowly give out and gradually it will get closer and closer to my hands until I grasp it, and snap it open, and release everything good I've been hoping for. But until that happens there is a voice inside me that says I can't do anything useful, and can't be anything, and can't say anything that is not ugly and destructive.'

'But you are not ugly and destructive,' I said. 'You are beautiful and really smart.' I cringed after I said that because usually when I say nice things to her she gets angry and hits me with her stick.

'I'm only sure of one thing,' she said with conviction. 'I'm mean. You know I can be awful. I am to my mother and I am to you, and I was awful at blind-girl school too.'

'It hurts me when you hit me with the stick,' I said. 'But it hurts me more when you say mean things because they stay inside me and lash out over and over again and I can't get out of their way.'

'Well, I'm not making excuses for how I am,' she continued, 'but let me tell you that it's bizarre to live a life where you cry black tears, and throw up black vomit, and pee black pee, and have emotions that are like black tides raising and lowering me as if I'm just a small rowboat at the mercy of storms I cannot see.

Believe me, when the tide of anger rises within me an ocean of raging black waves beats me and everything around me against a black shore.'

'What about the tide of happiness?' I asked.

'That tide rarely arrives,' she said with regret. 'But occasionally it does and the black ocean around the box seems at rest, like ripples of fur on a sleeping animal – happiness for me is still black but somehow it feels warmer.'

'Like Carter Junior,' I said. 'No matter how nutty I feel he always makes me feel better.'

'Yes,' she said, 'babies always make me float along on a high tide of happiness. They can't see that I'm blind, and even if they could they wouldn't care.' She reached towards me and tapped the air like when I search for a light switch in the dark. 'Give him to me.'

I bent over and picked Carter Junior up and pressed him to her shoulder and she closed her arms around him and held him tightly, then drew him to her face and sniffed the crown of his head.

'As a child,' she said a little more gently, 'once I discovered the black box inside the cavern of my mind I imagined that my whole past was in that box. And maybe in the past there was a time I could see, I thought – when I was a happy tiny bean inside my mother and growing like a sponge soaking up all the blood and oxygen and food and love. If I could see a dim light inside her before I was born, then in the box are memories deeply hidden of that time when everything around me was coloured blood-red. If the black box would open maybe those red memories would be released and join my black world, and then my world would take shape with red on black instead of black on black. If I just had one other colour. Just one! Then by contrast I could stand on a stage in my mind where I am red and only my shadow is black. Then I could see myself in all my greatness and I would make anger the smallest part of me.'

As she spoke her expressions changed and Carter Junior's expressions changed just like he was a little sock puppet on her hand. He mimicked every true feeling without understanding a word she was saying.

'But red on black, or white on black or orange or green – it doesn't matter,' she continued. 'The colours in my rainbow will always be black. So now I'm just all words inside, and sounds and feelings and smells and tastes but no colours. Words are my colours. They paint everything for me, but only as words. I love words, but at times I just wish I could hold an apple in my hand and see that it was red. With my hands I can feel the outline of things – I just wish I could colour within those lines.'

I felt like a black apple that had fallen out of her tree. But the more I watched her, the more all of Carter Junior's orange glow inside me began to darken until I felt as if the sun was sinking instead of rising.

I looked at Carter Junior and he started to squirm in her arms. 'You are having angry thoughts again,' I said to Olivia.

'How can you tell?' she replied.

'Carter Junior feels what you feel. I think you need to put that black box into a time-out and give him a kiss while I go into the house and change my meds,' I said. 'You are upsetting both of us.'

But before I left I picked up a little piece of the pizza crust that Carter Junior had dropped on the grass. I roughed it up between my fingers, then as quietly as possible I sprinkled the crumbs into the nest of hair that Olivia had made for the birds.

I looked at her determined face. It was set

exactly the same way as when I first stepped out the back door. Who knows what she was thinking about, but I knew what I was thinking.

'I'll be back in a minute,' I said.

10

SMELLS LIKE HOPE

When I walked into the house the phone was
ringing. I picked it up in the kitchen.

It was Mom.

'Joey,' she whispered. 'Joey, is that you?'

Just from her voice I could tell she wasn't on
her way back home.

'Yes, Mom,' I replied. 'It's me.' I reached up
into a kitchen cabinet and removed a patch.

'Joey, is it you? Really?' she asked.

'Yes,' I said. 'Really.'

'Good,' she said, then her voice dropped
down real low. 'Joey, how is the baby?'

'Fine,' I said. 'Really.'

'Do you see him?' she said.

'Who?' I asked.

'The baby,' she replied. 'Can you see him with your eyes?'

I looked out the kitchen window. Olivia had adjusted her hopeful Statue of Liberty pose. She had one arm up like a tree branch and the other wrapped around Carter Junior, who was happily settled under her arm with his head on her shoulder.

'Yes, Mom,' I replied. 'He's fine.'

'Well, keep an eye on him at all times,' she said. 'Because *he* was just here, Joey. Your dad. And he wants the baby. He thought Carter Junior was with me and he dressed up in a disguise as a doctor and came into my room when I was sleeping. He came to steal Carter Junior but the nurse told him that my baby is being cared for at home. He's after him, Joey. Keep an eye out and don't let that man in the house.'

'If you were sleeping, how did you know it was him?' I asked, because she had been making up a lot of stuff.

'Because the nurse said the man had the face of a *monster*,' she whispered. 'Frankenstein's monster. So it has to be your dad because of what he did to his face, so don't let him in the house whatever you do.'

After Dad's bad face surgery, he could look like anything. 'I won't let him near Carter Junior,' I said, still looking out the window. Carter Junior was tightly clamped under Olivia's arm.

'Don't open the door for anyone,' she warned me. 'Promise.'

'Nobody but Mr Fong,' I said, and changed the subject. 'Mom, when can I come visit you?' I asked. 'I miss you. And Carter Junior misses you.'

'You can't,' she replied. 'You can't leave the house. He'll be waiting for you. He'll sneak up on you like a monster and snatch the baby.'

'Will he steal me?' I asked, and the question was so odd inside me because half of me was scared of being stolen and the other half wanted to be stolen – stolen by my own dad who wanted me too.

'I don't think he'll take you,' she said. 'He just wants Carter Junior.'

'Because he's not broken like I am,' I said. 'Like you said I was.'

'I was sick when I said that,' she replied.

'But you weren't wrong,' I said. 'I am broken, because you know what I'm doing now? I'm putting on a new med patch, which you hid from me. I have to take meds every morning. That's like cheating at being OK. Like faking that I'm as good as new when really I'm like something broken, like a boy made out of glass that you step on then glue back together but he's still worthless. I'm not OK. I'm a mess.'

I couldn't slap my new patch on fast enough. I could feel myself getting all worked up and my words were racing way out in front of my brain and even though I was standing still the thoughts were spinning in my head so fast I was dizzy like I was on a fairground ride, and I was thinking that I was saying angry stuff like Olivia did and I didn't like it in her and now I didn't like it in my own self. Just then a single roach ran by and I got so angry I slapped it as hard as I could. I could feel its back cover crack and its guts splat out against the stinging palm of my hand. I looked around to see if I could find another one. I felt like waking them all up in their little Roach Motel beds and then rubbing them all out like a roach-killing gangster.

'Joey,' Mom said quietly as I rubbed my hand

on the back of my trousers after almost licking it. 'Are you OK? Really OK? And Carter Junior? Is he OK?'

'I'm sorry, Mom,' I said, but my heart was racing. 'I just got a little carried away but I'm OK now. Really. And Carter Junior is OK. I'm just sorry I said what I said, but I'm over it. Please don't feel bad.'

'Be careful,' she said. 'I have to go.' In the background I could hear a nurse or somebody calling her name.

'Are you feeling better?' I asked.

'Yes,' she said, and I could hear the genuine *yes* in her voice, as if she believed in what she was saying.

'Well, be pawzzz-i-tive,' I said in a wide-eyed way.

'We'll make this work,' she said quickly. 'The doctor said it's good for me to rest and talk my way through the bad stuff. And guess what? I'm on meds too!'

'When are you coming back?' I asked.

'I'm working on it,' she said quickly. 'Gotta run.'

Then she was gone. It was like someone had taken the phone out of her hand and hung up on me. I tried to imagine what might've happened. I could only imagine a picture of her walking down a long hospital hallway. She seemed in the middle of nowhere. Or was it halfway to home? I could feel her coming and going at the same time.

I looked out the window to make sure that someone hadn't taken Carter Junior out of Olivia's grip. But the baby was still there. And then he had company.

As Olivia kept her one-armed pose as the Statue of Liberty for Blind Girls a sparrow landed on her head and began to peck at the pizza crumbs. Then another dropped down next to it. And another, and in a few seconds her head was covered with a crown of frisky sparrows all nipping at the crumbs in her hair.

I could see it, but Olivia could feel it and her beaming face showed it. She smiled the biggest smile I had ever seen on her face, and the birds flapped their wings and danced on their springy legs, and when they finished getting every crumb they took flight and circled around her in a spiral up above the trees and then higher like a spraying fountain of birds and as they flew even higher I closed my eyes and had an oracle's vision. I could see that the birds had plucked and plucked at Olivia's head until they plucked that black box right out of her mind and then they flew into the air as high as the clouds and let it drop down in front of her and smash open and all her hopes and dreams were set free, and all the flames and anger turned into ashes and blew away. I could only hope I was seeing what she was feeling.

When I walked outside and stood next to her she was still smiling. It was almost as big a smile as the first time she had kissed me. But that only happened once.

'Did you see them?' she asked excitedly.

'Yes,' I said, 'it was great.'

'Did they make a nest?' she asked.

'They left a note behind,' I said, and pretended to pluck it out of her hair. 'It says, *Will lay eggs next year and start a family.*'

'You goofball,' she said, beaming.

'I wish I had a camera because then I could show you how happy you looked when they were on your head.' And then the moment I said that I cringed because I had done it again. 'I'm sorry,' I quickly said, and flinched because I expected to get a swat from her stick. 'I was being stupid about you seeing a picture.'

'It's OK,' she said. 'I'm sorry I've been mean because I really want to be nicer. And it's special times like this when the birds aren't afraid of me and I have a sleeping baby in my arms that I become so happy I forget that I can't see.'

'That's funny,' I said, 'because when I'm really happy and close my eyes I forget that I *can* see.'

'You don't have to see to feel happiness,' she said. 'When I hold this baby in my arms I don't see that black box. I just feel him and I can hold him to my ear and hear his heartbeat. I can smell him and kiss him and put his little fingers in my mouth. All I feel for this little Pigza is hope and love and happiness, and if you put all those feelings together it is like I have a bouquet of flowers in my heart that seem so real I can hold them in my hand and sniff them and smell their perfume.' She held Carter Junior up to her nose and took a deep breath and slowly exhaled. 'When you are blind, the heart sees the truth,' she said, and looked up towards the top of our tree where the birds had cascaded down and re-gathered.

Then I remembered something that Mrs Fabian had said in class. 'Did you know that the most famous Greek oracles were blind? The best one was named Tiresias who the goddess

Athena blinded because he saw her bathing naked, but then she felt bad for blinding him and gave him the power to understand the voices of the birds – and Athena was the one that gave him a blind person's stick.'

Olivia didn't say anything to me. Her ear was tilted towards the tree and she was listening to what the birds were saying. They must have been telling jokes because she was laughing.

11
DING-DOG!

I'm sitting on a living-room chair playing with Carter Junior on my lap and I'm staring at the doorknob of the front door because I'm waiting for Mr Fong to deliver our nightly pizza. But ever since Mom called I've been afraid. There's a good chance that when the doorbell rings it will be my scary dad arriving to stir up trouble. I should have been in a good mood because I talked with my mom and she said she was feeling better and that we'd work everything out, which I think means she'll come home at the end of her programme and we'll all get back to normal. That put a smile on my face and made me feel pawzzz-i-tive deep inside. But after a long while of sitting in front of the door waiting for the doorbell to ring, I began to remember when only my grandma and I lived together in this house and my mom had run off with my dad.

Grandma used to make me get bathed and dressed up in my Tasmanian devil pyjamas and sit by myself in a chair by the window. My dud meds were not working well back then and I was so squirmy and wired that to make me calm down my grandma used to say that if I sat perfectly still in the chair and kept my hands in my lap and didn't kick the legs of the chair or wiggle or pluck out my hair, then my mother would sneak a peek through the window and see that I was not a broken boy, and she'd clasp her hands over her heart and walk up the porch steps and knock on the door and come back to her good boy with open arms. How I loved waiting for my mom to find me, and for a little while I sat in that chair as still as a good-boy statue.

But after a while, no matter how hard I tried to lock my feet around the legs of the chair and hook my fingers under the rim of the seat, I'd slowly lose my grip and start to squirm. I'd grit my teeth and hold my breath and try not to wiggle even one finger, but after a while that good boy my mom wanted would start kicking the chair legs and pulling out his hair and slipping out of his seat like Houdini escaping his chains. I couldn't stop myself. I'd flop down onto the floor and laugh crazily and clap my hands together and *arf-arf-arf* like a seal until Grandma would stand over me and say, 'Forget it! You blew it! Your mom peeked in the window and saw what kind of bad boy you are. Now she's never coming back for you. Ever.'

That would just kill me, and I'd hang my head and cry and cry and beg for a second chance, and my grandma would soften up and say, 'OK, I'll call your mother and ask for a second chance and we'll try again tomorrow to sit still.' But then we'd just do it all over the next day and I'd lose control like I always did. I never could sit still, and my mother never did peek in the window. She wasn't even in town. Sitting in the chair was all a trick my grandma cooked up to try to make me settle down while giving herself a breather so she could smoke her cigarettes and watch TV in peace.

And now here I am again, sitting on a chair in the living room, only this time I'm not facing the window and waiting for my mom to see how good I am. This time I'm facing the door and I'm waiting for my dad to show up like the Big Bad Wolf to blow our house down and spoil things for the perfect little piggy Pigza. So I just sit with Carter Junior curled up on my lap and stare at the door so I can stare at something solid, which makes me feel solid. Usually when I get all worked up and fidgety and out of control it's for all the wrong reasons, but now I feel wired and on task at the same time, like my face is the engine of a train speeding fearlessly through a tunnel, and it is the most powerful feeling I have ever had.

I was leaning way forward in my chair and Olivia was on the couch tapping her stick on the floor like she was counting down the seconds to a head-on collision.

'Remember all your talk about a black box?' I said without taking my eyes off the door.

'How could I forget?' she grumbled. 'It's always blocking my beautiful black view.'

'Well, you made me see something I had never seen before,' I said.

'What's that?' she asked.

'This whole house is a black box,' I said slowly. 'When I close my eyes all I see is this crazy house in my head. I wish it was full of hopes and dreams, but instead everything bad happens here – in fact we're like a family-in-a-black-box.'

'Then open your eyes and forget about it,' she advised. 'Lord knows, I wish I could.'

'When I open my eyes I just see that front door and I know the next time it opens, my life is going to change,' I said.

'Change how?' she asked.

'I'm going to *fix* my family,' I said with determination. 'I'm going to change things around here.'

'You?' she asked.

'Yeah, me,' I replied. 'Me. I'm going to do it. That's my dream.'

'You *are* dreaming,' she remarked. 'How can you change your family when they won't change themselves?'

'I don't know yet,' I said. 'But part of the answer is on the other side of the door.'

'Good luck with that plan,' she replied with scepticism. 'Let me say that as an oracle, your dream of fixing this family is a nightmare! Believe me, you Pigzas are as blind to being a family as I am to seeing across this room.'

'I almost fixed them,' I said, staring at the

door like it was a target. 'I was close last year. I thought we could forgive each other for being so mean and find a way to come together as a happy family. But then everyone spun out of control and went their own crazy way. Dad ran off with his zombie face-lift, and Mom had the baby and got drifty and sad, and I fell into a rut. I used to sit in my closet with the lights off and cry. It was the worst crying too. It was like broken crying for a broken dream. I'd sit on my floor with my eyes glazed over and my chin sagging down and a weird sound like a floppy broken word tumbling around in my mouth, just kind of turning over and over like a flat tyre going nowhere. That broken dream knocked the air out of me.'

'And now you are going to try fixing them again?' she asked, sounding doubtful. 'Remember when you said I was blind, and blind girls couldn't take vacations?'

'Yes,' I said.

'Well, you are blinder than I am. I can walk out that door free as a bird but you are completely trapped in this mess.'

'Don't be angry,' I said. 'This really is hard for me even as I'm trying to feel pawzzz-i-tive this time. Last time I was too angry to forgive everyone. I just wanted to hurt them. But this time I just need to remember my special gift – if I can feel all the good that's in them, then I think it will work out.'

'Well, I've been waiting for the door on my black box to open all my life,' she said, sounding unconvinced. 'And you know what? Even if I open that box, my anger may never go away.'

'I hate to put it this way,' I said, 'but your own anger is blinding you to your gifts.'

She frowned at that thought and pointed her stick at the door. 'Before *that* ding-dog dinner bell rings I have a prediction,' she announced.

'Let's hear it,' I replied.

'Tonight's pizza,' she said in a spooky oracle voice, 'is going to be a *special* gift.'

'It will be the same as always,' I said with a big smile, because I loved pizza. 'We don't even call in the order. Every night it's an extra-cheesy, extra-red-sauce pizza. Even if we aren't home, Mr Fong leaves it on the front porch. It's exactly the same, which is how I like it. I don't like surprises.'

'Well, tonight it is going to be different,' she said. 'When you open the pizza box it's going to be surprisingly different.'

And then the doorbell rang.

'Right on time,' she said. 'Answer it. I'm starving.'

I wasn't. I stared at the door and uncoiled from my chair like a cold snake, and with Carter Junior pressed tightly against one shoulder I reached for the doorknob with my free hand.

'Go on,' she said. 'Get the special pizza.'

I took a deep breath. 'Ding-dog!' I said to the door. 'Round one!'

'Oh, and give me the baby first,' Olivia cried out.

I should have. Instead, I slid the dead bolt to one side and twisted the doorknob. Then I pulled the door towards me.

It was dark out and our porch light was busted, but from the light in the living room I could see he was wearing a red-and-white pizza delivery jumpsuit and holding out an Antonio's Pizzeria box. He had a baseball cap with the brim pulled down low, but it was my dad – only it looked as if he had an extra-cheesy, extra-red-sauce pizza smeared across his scarred-up face.

'Where is Mr Fong?' I asked, and eased back a step.

Muy malo,' he said in a fake Spanish voice.

I turned and glanced at Olivia. 'Catch!' I was going to shout, and toss Carter Junior past the open door and into her arms. In my mind throwing the baby didn't seem dangerous at all. He would float through the air like a pitcher of milk that didn't spill.

I should have done that. Even if she missed him, I still should have tried it. But instead, something in me wanted to give Dad one more chance. I could still feel that faint spark of goodness inside him where he kept it hidden – even from himself. So I turned back to face him.

'Dad!' I said, and cradled Carter Junior with both arms and held him out a bit for Dad to see his sweet face. 'He looks like you – don't you think?'

I was also going to say that Carter Junior looked a little bit like everyone in our whole family – even the dogs – when Dad suddenly shouted out, 'Pizza delivery!' In an instant the pizza box sprang forward and the front edge popped me across the nose. When I flinched and turned my face to one side he got his quick hands on Carter Junior.

It happened so fast. I was strong but he was stronger. 'Let go of Junior!' I think I yelled. He did, but then he grabbed my wrists and tugged me across the porch. When we reached the steps I started to tip forward with Carter Junior in my arms. I twisted my shoulders round, and as I toppled onto my back and sledded down the steps he plucked Carter Junior from my arms like he was picking a melon.

Carter Junior went off like a siren. Dad tucked him under his arm and ran down Plum Street.

By then I had flipped back onto my feet and started chasing after him.

'Stop! Baby thief!' I hollered, then regretted saying that because I didn't want the cops to get involved because of my promise to Mom.

Dad turned to see how far I was behind him and his hat flew off. The back of his head looked like a thick collar of monkey fur.

I've always been a fast runner and I knew I could catch him, but it was how to tackle him without hurting Carter Junior that worried me, so I just stayed right behind him.

'Stop!' I shouted. 'It's me! Joey! Your other son.'

But he didn't stop. He ran like he was a cartoon caveman character, only moving from the knees down.

I got right behind him and reached out thinking that if I could snag his back pockets and hang on I could slow him down without knocking him over. But when I snatched at him he dodged to one side and my fingers hooked his side pocket and ripped it down the seam. Some coins sprayed out, and I reached after him again as we turned the corner onto Chestnut Street. Dad leaped into the street just when a car pulled out of Quips Pub. The headlights shone on us and the driver hit the brakes. We didn't slow down. Dad cut across the street and sprinted towards the dark path between two houses. I was still right behind him and Carter Junior was screaming in a way I had never heard a baby scream before. He was so scared, which made me feel scared, but I didn't have time for that now. I had to be brave for him, and maybe if he could feel my courage he would be brave too.

We passed between the houses and crossed Franklin Street and kept going.

'Stop,' I kept saying. 'Stop. You are scaring him!'

Dad didn't slow down. It was like he had just robbed a bank. I guess he ran so hard because stealing a kid is worse than stealing money.

I followed him into the dark yard between two more houses and neither of us saw the clotheslines. The first one missed the baby and got Dad around the neck and his feet shot forward. He hit the damp ground on his back, and as he slid forward on the slick grass he held Carter Junior up in the air to keep him safe. That was my chance. I speeded up, and just when I reached out to pluck little Carter Junior back from Dad's arms I hit the second clothesline. My head snapped back and my feet flew out and I landed flat on my back, but I was in luck. Dad went sliding on his bottom and ended up pushing over the side of a kid's paddling pool. There was a big splash. I thought Carter Junior must be dead because he wasn't howling any more. I just grazed the side of the pool, and when I dug my heels into the grass and hopped up Dad was on his feet but he was not holding the baby. He was staring in disbelief at his hands as if they had just magically swallowed Carter Junior.

'Where's the baby?' I yelled.

'I don't know,' he said breathlessly, and then, when he saw me leaping towards him like a mad flying squirrel, he spun away and ran for the darkest part of the back yard.

'Wait!' I hollered. 'Get back here! Help me find the baby!' But he disappeared into a thick hedge that crackled as branches shivered and snapped, and after more clawing he dropped out into the parking lot on the other side. He picked himself up.

'Your mother's in the hospital!' he yelled. 'That baby needs his father.'

'She's sick,' I said as I looked wildly around for my little Buddha-Baby, 'but she's getting better.'

'I'll be back for my boy!' he said, panting like a wolf.

'What about me?' I asked. 'When are you coming back for me?'

'When you learn how to listen,' he said harshly. Then he slowly loped away since he knew I couldn't follow because I had to take care of Carter Junior.

I turned away from the quivering hedge and heard a sound from the kiddie pool. Carter Junior was sitting on his bottom and kicking his chubby legs to the side and spinning in a circle of murky water and dead leaves.

I snatched him up and held him in my arms and kissed him all over his wet head. I knew that if something bad happened to Carter

Junior, nobody would blame me – but they'd blame Mom and that wouldn't be fair because she was busy getting stronger and I was the one who was supposed to protect him. But he was fine.

I carried him back towards Plum Street. When I passed the spot where I had seen the coins fly out of Dad's ripped pocket I squatted down and picked them up because we could always use the money. And then I spotted something more valuable. It was the macramé key chain I'd made him in second grade, and there was just one key on it, and it had to be his apartment key. It was an old brass key, dull and dirty, and even under the streetlight it didn't shine. I put it into my pocket.

'Come on, Carter Junior,' I whispered hopefully. 'We have some thinking to do. But first, let's get you cleaned up.'

When I got to the house Olivia was pacing back and forth on the front porch. 'I'll kill him,' she hissed, while swinging her stick around like she was fighting all three of the Musketeers at once. 'I'll *fix* him!' she snapped. 'I'll chop him to bits and feed him to vultures.'

'It could have been worse,' I said. 'We still have the baby.'

'You better forget about *fixing* up the Pigza household,' she said in a scornful voice. 'Just fix the locks. He's a menace!'

'You don't make this easier,' I said.

'It's not my job to make you feel happy,' she replied. 'Rule number two at my school is that every student is responsible for their own happiness – and that goes double for *adults*.'

When we went back into the house I took Carter Junior down to the bathroom and sat him in the tub and turned on the warm water and gave him a splash bath and then dried him off and rubbed Vaseline on his raw bottom so he wouldn't get a rash. I put him in a fresh nappy and took him back out to the living room. When I got there Pablo and Pablita were growling at the door and then growling at me, and then growling at the door again. At first I thought Dad might have snuck back, but then I realized the pizza was still in the box on the porch.

I handed Carter Junior to Olivia. 'If you and I were married,' Olivia said to me as she kissed his head, 'and this was our baby, I would do anything to protect him.'

'That's rule number one in the real world,' I said.

'Yeah, but Pigzas don't live in the real world,' she replied.

That was so true because if we were the real world then the *whole* world was in trouble.

But the good news is the pizza was fine. It was sort of upside down and scrunched up in the box like an accordion, but because it was Antonio's extra-cheesy with extra red sauce it tasted the same anyway. I chopped up a couple of pieces for the dogs and Carter Junior gummed a piece, and Olivia and I ate like we were maniacs because we were so nervous.

When we finished Olivia was smiling.

'What's so funny?' I asked.

'My blind-girl oracle prediction was accurate,' she said. 'This pizza is *really* special.'

I had to agree – even though it was the exact same pizza Mr Fong always delivered.

12

THE SECRET KEY

That night I went to bed with the key in my mouth. I was sucking on it like Carter Junior sucking on his thumb. It tasted like a damp old penny you find under a rock, all mossy and dirty-tasting. It was salty, and when I had worked the crud and flavour off one side I turned it over with my tongue and sucked on the other side. I fell asleep with that key in my mouth and when I woke up it was still there. I must have been sucking on it all night because when I pulled it out in the morning it was no longer mossy and dull. I had stripped everything off the key and now it was as bright and shiny as a brass button.

I hopped out of bed and went into the kitchen. Olivia had been up. The pizza box was open. The last slice was gone but Dad had not come back to eat it. When I looked out the window Olivia was back to posing in the yard. Her crumb-covered right hand was held up by her ear while the birds fluttered mid-air and darted down in turns to peck crumbs off her palm. In her other arm she held Carter Junior over her shoulder as if he was a sack of rice. He was smacking his lips as he gummed that last slice of special pizza. A bird hovered over his head.

I strolled out to see her, and the birds scattered into the trees.

'You ruined it,' she said, hearing me.

'Ruined what?' I asked.

'I was thinking about Helen Keller,' she said thoughtfully, 'and I was telling myself to count my blessings because I can hear birds, and she could not, and I bet if she could have heard birds chirping she'd have been thrilled.'

'That's very pawzzz-i-tive,' I said in a hugely positive way so she could hear my hugely positive smile.

'Mom always said to be grateful for what you have,' she said. 'I do try, but sometimes I lose hope.'

'I know what you mean,' I replied. 'I should be happy with just having Mom and Carter Junior but I want Dad too – as nutty as he is.'

'Well, you can have your dad,' she said. 'Just give me Carter Junior because he is a good influence on me. It's impossible to be a grump when I'm with him.'

'He is the perfect Buddha-Baby positive Pigza,' I remarked.

'Yep,' she said, and kissed his head. 'Babies make me happy.'

'What about me?'

'You make me happy when you don't act like a baby,' she said.

I reached out and pressed the key into her hand. 'As for the imperfect Pigza,' I said, 'he dropped his apartment key last night.'

'And I bet you're insane enough to try to find him,' she said without enthusiasm.

'Every door in town,' I replied with conviction. 'Once an idea gets inside me it's like I become the idea in motion, and the only thing that will fix me will be to fix him or my head will explode.'

'But while you are out looking for him, he knows where to look for you. Does he have a key to this house?' she asked.

'Mom had the locks changed,' I said, 'and got a meat cleaver.'

'Then I'll stay here with Carter Junior,' she said. 'But if he breaks through that cardboard front door I'll get the meat cleaver and fix his face my way.'

'You could only make it better,' I said.

Just then the kitchen phone rang. I swiped the key from Olivia's hand and ran back inside the house. I didn't have to be an oracle to know who it would be. I picked up the phone and could hear his clammy breathing. 'You have my key,' he said. 'Give it back.'

'You ruined our family,' I said. 'Give that back.'

'I'll leave you alone if you give me the key,' he offered.

'You'll never leave us alone,' I replied. 'You always say you will, but you never do.'

'Show me some respect – I'm your *dad*,' he replied.

'Earn some,' I said right back. 'Nobody hates you. We're just afraid of you, which is confusing because we love you.'

'Just be a man and bring the key to Antonio's,' he said roughly.

I was going to yell back, *Just be a man and say you love us*, but he hung up on me first. I hate being hung up on.

Now I really wanted to *fix* him. Just then I noticed the microwave door was open and a gang of roaches were gathered inside. I slammed the door shut and hit the popcorn button. I stuck my fingers in my ears. Even though roaches don't scream I can hear their pretend screams.

When Dad tells me to be a man he's really telling himself to be one, and when he says he is happy to be away from us I can hear that he is not. I think he is screaming to grow up and come back to us – the only thing is, he never listens to himself.

I got dressed and said goodbye to Olivia and Carter Junior, then headed out. I wasn't sure what I was going to do when I saw him so I figured I better think of a plan.

Over the summer while Mom was so depressed in bed and holed up in her room with Carter Junior, I spent a lot of time out of the house trying to come up with a plan to find Dad. At first I just started running up and down the streets as if I might bump into him. I wasn't even sure I would talk to him, but I imagined playing something like tag where I ran by and slapped him on the back and shouted, 'Tag! You're it!' and then I'd turn round and blast off like a giggling maniac and he'd chase after me and we'd both zigzag back and forth across the street as if we were lacing up a tall boot. Finally he would follow me into the house and tag me – but I wouldn't let him go. He'd be trapped in there like a wild horse in a corral and I could tame him and then we could run through the town together with me riding on his back and he'd be totally under my control.

That plan never worked. As I continued to roam the streets I saw a lot of Dad-duds I thought were him. I'd run by a diner and glance in the windows. There were always a lot of blank-looking guys hunched over cups of coffee and sandwiches but none with Dad's patch-work face. When I passed a corner store that sold lottery tickets I always gave the guys slouching in the doorway a second look because playing the lottery was Dad's favourite game.

I'd run up and down the lines of homeless men waiting for a hand-out from the shelter at

Saint Francis. I jogged by a man stretched out on a sheet of folded cardboard. He had a filthy scarf loosely wrapped around his face. Through the opening I could see two eyes balled up into small dark fists. He was about the right scrawny size as Dad, and as I circled him he unwrapped his stiff scarf and glared at me.

But it wasn't my dad. 'Wrong face,' I yelped as he snatched at my sneaker with one hand like it was the edge of a cliff.

I felt bad for him but he did give me an idea. I wrapped white toilet paper around my head and kept it tight with a few rubber bands. I separated a few of the edges around my eyes so I could see, and lifted a little flap under the tip of my nose so I could breathe, and I opened a gap for my mouth. I didn't want much of me to show. I got some ketchup and mixed it with garden dirt and rubbed that on the toilet paper to make it look as if I had been bleeding and dizzy and had fallen down and was hurt. This is what I figured Dad must have looked like at some time.

Then I got a piece of cardboard out of the trash and with a marker I wrote in big letters:

HIT MY HEAD!
LOST MY MEMORY.
DO YOU KNOW WHERE I LIVE?

I walked downtown to an old section by the farmers' market and held up the sign. I wasn't asking for money. I was just asking how I might find my dad. But no matter how many streets I ran up and down and how many windows I looked into or how long I sat pretending to have amnesia, I still couldn't find Dad or anyone who knew where he was. He had vanished behind that new face, which was so repulsive that people wanted to forget it.

But then, just when I thought I'd never find him, he came to my front door, and now I had his house key and knew he worked at Antonio's Pizzeria. All I needed was the other piece of the key – the lock.

So I jogged down Chestnut Street to Antonio's parking lot and crouched down behind a car bumper and spied on him just as he had been spying on us. Every few minutes a big hat would slowly jut out of the side kitchen door and the dark shadow of his face would stare down the street as if I was dumb enough to show up and stick the key into his hand.

After a while he stepped outside and was smoking a cigarette with another delivery guy when his boss leaned out the door and said, 'Hey, Pigza, run these pizzas up to the college dorm.'

Dad snuffed his cigarette out on the bottom of his shoe and hustled into the kitchen. He came out with a stack of pizzas and got into the Antonio's delivery truck.

Once he was out of sight I trotted over to the kitchen door where the other guy was still smoking.

'Is Mr Fong around?' I asked.

'He only works nights,' the guy said.

'Oh,' I said to myself. I was hoping Mr Fong could tell me where Dad lived.

'Well, do you know where that other pizza delivery guy lives?' I asked, trying out Plan B.

'Why do you want to know?' he asked.

'I'm his kid,' I said proudly. 'Can't you tell? I look just like him.' I made a bug-eyed, bucktooth, silly face because no matter how hard I tried I never could make a scary face.

'You must be pulling my leg,' the guy remarked, and began to laugh out loud. 'Pigza has a kid? Women won't open the door when he delivers. If you were his kid you'd already be dead from fright. Just looking at him almost gives me a heart attack!'

'But do you know where he lives?' I said, feeling a little sad about what he had just said about Dad.

'Does he know you are his kid?' he asked.

'Just as much as I know he's my dad,' I replied.

He blew out a final puff of smoke and flicked the butt into the parking lot with a little smile on his face as if he had thought of something clever. 'Try Alley Oop Street. Alley Oop is his nickname. We stopped there once after a delivery and he ran into his place for something. I didn't pay attention to the number but I remember the street name because he was singing that silly caveman song about Alley Oop. You know, *He's got a big ugly club and a head fulla hairuh, Alley Oop, oop, oop-oop.*'

'Alley Oop?' I repeated.

'Alley O. Over by Buchanan Park,' he said, and pointed. 'Offa West End Ave, like Alley A, Alley N, Alley O.'

'Oh,' I said. 'I got it.'

I took off before Dad returned. Buchanan Park was a few blocks away from where I went to school, for one day so far. When I reached

139

Alley O, I paused and stood behind a tree. The alley was long and unpaved and either side of it was lined with old brick garages that had been turned into apartments. I took the key out of my pocket. It was a Yale key, so I was looking for a Yale lock. I just got myself revved up and marched over to the side door of the first garage. It was a Yale lock but my key didn't fit. I dashed over to the next garage side door and tried it. Nope. I tried the next one. Nope. I looked over my shoulder to see if anyone was paying attention to me. Nope. I went to the next garage. Nope. The next. Nope. And by the time I finished one whole side of the alley I was feeling like my chances of finding his apartment were either half better, or half worse.

I tackled down the other side. Nope. Nope. Nope. I was starting to fidget like a squirrel that forgot where he hid his acorn.

Then, 'Yes!' I hissed after the key slid into a lock, and when I turned it to the right it kept turning and then the tumblers rolled over and the door cracked open like an oyster.

Until that moment I had only thought about finding his door. But what would I do when I was in the house? What would I say to him if he came home?

I was feeling a little springy inside and realized I'd forgotten to change my patch this morning. I slapped my arm where I had my old patch just to wake it up, and called out, 'Carter?' I used his name like I was an old friend. 'Carter, old buddy. Are you home? I got some money for you.' I figured that last bit would get him out. But no, so I stepped forward and pulled the door behind me.

On the hallway wall was a peg with a doctor's coat and white surgeon's mask hanging down. I crept along that dark hallway, not knowing what real monster mask was waiting to reach out for me. I turned the corner but didn't see him.

'Dad?' I called out. 'Are you here?' There was no answer so I kept going. I entered the little kitchen. For some reason I opened the refrigerator. All the food was neat and tidy and perfectly wrapped up. On the windowsill he had lined up a row of apple cores and the room smelled sweet like rotting apples. Mom did the same. I went into his bedroom and his bed was perfectly made up. I opened his closet and all his shirts and trousers were ironed. Even his socks were folded over hangers and hanging up. I opened a drawer and all his vests were folded.

On a little desk all his mail was sorted out in neat stacks and there was a soup can full of pencils and pens. There was a framed picture of Carter Junior that was taken when he was born, and the little blue imprint of his foot on a piece of paper.

I looked around for more pictures and noticed a small room off his room, like a closet without a door. I stuck my head round the corner and that's when I saw the crib. It was brand-new and perfectly made up with clean sheets and a baby blanket and stuffed animals. The walls of the room were freshly painted, and in one corner was a changing table with nappies and cream and a soft night-light and everything else a new baby would need.

I reached into the crib and pulled out a little pillow. *Carter Junior* was hand-stitched on the front of it. Dad must have imagined living with Carter Junior and feeling all the love and happiness of starting over in a new house with a new baby and a new heart and hopes and dreams. But no matter what his dream was I couldn't just let him take the piece of Pigza he wanted and throw away the rest of us.

I don't know what came over me, but I kicked my shoes off and climbed into the small cage of that perfect crib. There was a mobile of farm animals attached to the rail. I wound it up and a scratchy voice sang, *'Old MacDonald had a farm, E-I-E-I-O.'* And as the song played I curled up on my side and looked above me at the animals dancing in a circle like a halo over my head. I was cool so I opened the knitted blue blanket and pulled it up to my chin. When I was a baby I had a crib and a music box that played *'Twinkle, twinkle, little star, how I wonder what you are.'* Now I wondered what I had become because I was a boy but it suddenly felt so good to be the baby again.

I still had the key in my hand and I held it up to my mouth, but instead of the key I pushed my thumb between my lips. It tasted so good and dreamy and I was suddenly as tired as a newborn. I lowered my eyelids and sucked on my thumb until I slipped into a deep sleep like Goldilocks finding just the right bed. I wish I had slept like the ancient Greeks and had a dream that revealed what was going to happen next in my life, but when I suddenly woke up it was night and the apartment was dark and all I felt was fear that he would find me – the wrong Pigza boy – in Carter Junior's bed.

I grabbed the bars on the crib as if I was

trapped inside my own black box and in a panic I hopped out of the crib. I felt around and turned on the night-light. I pulled the sheets tight and smoothed them out as best I could with the flat of my hand. I folded up the blanket. Then I slipped my shoes on and slowly turned in a circle to make sure everything was the same as when I walked in. I hoped it was. I turned off the light and marched out of the little room, and through his bedroom and down the hall. It scared me to open his door because he could be an inch away from opening it himself with a new key, and if he was there he would grab me and the scare would hit me like lightning and I'd drop dead on the spot. But I had no other choice but to get out of there. I took a deep breath and turned the doorknob.

13

IN A HOLE

When I returned home I stood on the sidewalk and stared blankly at the flat front of my dark house. The corner streetlamps were on. The parking lot security lights at Quips Pub were on. Up and down the row of houses the porch lights showed off all the front doors, and the windows were checkered with lights turning off and on as the shadows of people shifted left and right behind the curtains. But my house stood in front of me like a black tooth in a broken smile.

'Don't panic,' I whispered to myself. 'She's a

blind oracle. She doesn't need to turn lights on to see what's going on. She has inner vision.'

That seemed sensible for about a second, and then I manically bolted up the steps, and when I yanked out my key I jammed it into the lock and turned it so hard the house could have flipped over onto its side. 'Olivia!' I hollered as I pushed the door open. 'Olivia?'

Only the dogs answered as they ran barking at me and punching their heads against my ankles like two angry fists. I fell down, then stood up and flicked the lights on. The house was a wreck. It was hard to know if someone had come in through the open back door and ransacked it or if it was just Olivia's mess because dropping things on the floor was her method of putting things away.

I dashed into the kitchen and got the meat cleaver out of the freezer. I hacked the air back and forth as I ran from room to room upstairs and downstairs, and then right away did the same thing again just in case a burglar was hiding the first time and I'd catch him the second time trying to sneak out. But no one was in the house except for me and the dogs and a sick feeling that something bad had happened.

Olivia and Carter Junior were gone and I

stood there hating myself because while I was sleeping like a thumb-sucking little baby in a crib they were taken away. They were stolen and I should have been home to protect them because just before Mom left she told me I was the man of the house and that I had to act like one and protect Carter Junior from Dad. But I didn't. Instead I fell asleep on the job and let her down and now everything was ruined.

I went to the kitchen. The cupboard door with my calendar on it was open. Mom was supposed to come home any day now and I wanted everything to be perfect for her but instead I was just making her life more miserable. I figured that when she came home I'd give her the meat cleaver and let her chop me up into a thousand Pigza pieces like I was some stupid boy roach.

I set the cleaver on the counter and picked up the telephone receiver to call the police. I wished I didn't have to be the man of the house. I wanted to be the old out-of-control Joey, which was me at my best and worst. I never had to care if I was good or bad or helpful or trouble. I wanted to be the fun Joey. The wild Joey. The laughing-like-a-hyena Joey. I'd love to be my old wired self again and be the number-one problem all day long and have everyone want to take care of me. But now I had to be the mature Joey, the think-before-you-speak Joey, the better-than-Dad Joey, the hold-the-fort-for-Mom Joey, the keep-the-baby-safe Joey, the answer-man-with-a-plan Joey.

But I didn't have a plan and I had to think of what I was going to tell the police, because if I didn't think about what I was going to say I knew I would just yell into the telephone, 'Help me! Help me! Help me!' about a thousand times in a row while I picked up the cleaver and chopped the entire kitchen to bits, and when the police showed up they'd find me with the bloody meat cleaver whittling my own head down into a red pencil point so I could write 'I'm helpless!' on the wall.

Settle down and practise what to say, Joey, I said to myself. *Remember, practice makes a perfect Pigza*. Do I tell the police that Mom is in the hospital because she doesn't want to hurt the baby, and my dad is trying to steal the baby, and I'm here taking care of the baby, with a blind girlfriend who loves the baby, and do I blurt out that now they are all missing and somehow it's totally my fault? Is that what I tell the police? It sounded crazy when I said it out loud to myself. Even the dogs looked at me like I was crazy, but I had to tell the police something because if I truly was the man of the house I had to start acting like one.

Then suddenly I heard *tap-tap-tap* up the front steps. The doorknob turned back and forth but the door was locked. Then there was a window rattling *thwack-thwack-thwack* on the front door.

I *loved* that sound!

'Coming!' I shouted, and tossed the telephone receiver in the sink.

'Hurry up!' she shouted, and there was something in her voice that made me afraid.

I ran into the living room and whipped the door open.

Olivia stood there with her empty arms hanging limply by her sides and shiny lines of blood from her cut-up knees running down her legs and into her muddy sneakers.

'I'm sorry,' she said, and lowered her head.

'Where's Carter Junior?' I asked breathlessly.

She trudged past me and heaved herself onto the couch and began to cry.

'Tell me,' I said. 'What's going on? Did Dad snatch him?'

'I lost the baby.'

I stared at her. 'What do you mean, *lost* the baby! You can lose a wallet or an umbrella but not a baby!' Then I anxiously grabbed her hand. 'What did Dad do?' I asked. 'Did he snatch him? Tell me!'

She sat hunched with her hands held stiffly against her face like a stopped clock. 'It was not your dad,' she quietly sobbed. 'It was all my fault. I'm the one who lost the baby.'

'How?' I shot back. 'How can you just lose a baby? They scream when you lose them, so you can instantly find them!'

'I don't know! At one moment I had him in the shopping trolley. And the next I stepped into a deep hole and he rolled away.'

She wasn't making any sense. 'Did you hit your head?' I asked. She sounded nutty.

'Just call the police,' she replied. 'He's gone.'

I went into the kitchen and pulled the receiver out of the sink, and took a deep breath.

Just then the doorbell rang.

'It's the police!' Olivia shouted.

'I didn't call them yet,' I yelled over my shoulder. 'It's somebody else!' I ran for the door with the dogs barking and running figure eights between my feet. Olivia was right behind me with her stick poking me in the back of the head.

'If it's your dad I'm going to kill him,' she threatened.

'Don't kill me by mistake,' I cried out.

I whipped open the door and jumped back into a karate pose.

It wasn't Dad.

'Pig-zah delivery!' Mr Fong cried out happily. And it really *was* a Pigza delivery. He had Carter Junior sitting on a warm pizza box and gumming a slice of extra-cheesy pizza. 'Baby-Buddha!' Mr Fong said, and patted Carter Junior on his round head.

'Where did you find him?' I asked, and picked him up and gave him a hug and kissed his sweet face and passed him to Olivia.

She dropped her stick and purred, 'My bundle of hope.' And she held him like she would never let him go.

'Baby-Buddha likes Pig-zah,' Mr Fong said. 'I find him in a shopping trolley in the pizza parking lot.'

I turned to Olivia. 'Were you on College Ave. when you lost him?' I asked.

'Yes,' she said. 'And I was going to take a left on Chestnut.'

'Pizza store on corner of College and Chestnut,' Mr Fong said. 'So I deliver the special Baby-Buddha Pig-zah pizza.'

Olivia bumped me with her hip and I moved aside as she stepped forward. 'I want to say thank you,' she said, and stuck out her hand. 'You just saved me from something worse than blindness. If Carter Junior disappeared, my life would be even darker because he is a light inside my heart.'

Mr Fong reached out and held her hand in both of his. He smiled. 'Don't lose baby again,' he warned her. 'I deliver pizza. People open their door and I see inside their house. Bad people out there – but good people in here. Keep the baby safe.' He patted her hand when he said 'good people in here', and that made me so proud to be a Pigza.

'Thank you,' Olivia said in a quiet voice.

Mr Fong turned and walked down the stairs. I didn't say anything to Olivia, but across the street I saw a shadow of a man hunched down and shifting like a monkey between two parked cars. Thank goodness Mr Fong had found Carter Junior first.

'Now let me change this nappy,' she said,

and took Carter Junior down the hall to the bathroom.

I locked the front door and took the pizza into the kitchen and picked up the meat cleaver and started to chop up a slice for the dogs. But I wasn't hungry and I don't think anyone else was either. So I closed the pizza box and went out to the living room to sit on the couch next to Olivia, who was holding the baby.

'I bet you are wondering what happened,' Olivia said, and started crying again.

'I'm wondering if you hit your head and lost your mind,' I replied.

'While you were gone your mother called the house,' she sobbed, 'and wanted to see Carter Junior and get him used to her before coming back home. She says the doctor has a big plan for how she can better help herself and the baby when she gets out. I thought visiting your mom would be a good idea,' she said, 'and it was. She really missed him, and when he saw her he was the perfect mother-loving Pigza.'

'Well?' I said impatiently. 'All this is good news but tell me again what happened to you and the baby.'

'After your mom called I put him in a shopping trolley like you had done and wheeled him over to the hospital. She is really doing great,' Olivia said. 'She's eager to come home. Of course, when she hears how I lost the baby she'll be sick all over again. It'll probably kill her, though I wish she would just kill me.'

'Don't worry about her,' I said. 'She lost me for a few years, so losing Carter Junior for a few hours is nothing.'

'It was all going so well,' she continued. 'We had a lovely visit. Then I had him in the shopping trolley on the way home, and we were both so happy, and I was singing a silly song to him when I stupidly tripped over something and fell sideways into a deep hole. I guess they were doing roadwork and left it open or something. Anyway, I was upside down in the hole and the trolley kept going. I heard it rattling down the hill, and then Carter Junior started screaming and I started screaming, 'My baby! My baby! Someone help me. Please help me!' And I really wanted help. I needed help, and for the first time in a long time I felt blind, and helpless, and afraid. And while I waited for someone to help me I promised myself that if Carter Junior could be found unharmed I'd stop being so mean and angry and dedicate my life to being more hopeful and loving.'

'But then what?' I begged. 'Didn't you climb out and run after him?'

'I couldn't,' she said. 'It took me a moment to work my way up onto my feet. The hole was deep and the sides kept crumbling down as I tried to claw my way up. I kept yelling but no one came to help me, and after a minute I couldn't hear Carter Junior or the trolley rattling away, and there I was stuck crying in that hole. It was like that awful black box in my mind finally opened up and swallowed me, and instead of being filled with hope it was filled with all my self-hatred, and I just felt like I was burning alive in that hole and I deserved it because I'm nothing but a *useless* blind girl.'

'You are not useless,' I said, and put my hands on her shoulders. 'Without you I'd be the useless one.'

'But I didn't have a clue where he was,' she blurted out, and threw her arms into the air. 'My greatest fear has always been that my greatest weakness will keep me from doing the one good thing I've always wanted to do – just take care of babies – and now I've lost one. Nothing could be worse. I wish you had called the police. I want them to arrest me. I'm nothing but trouble. I think I'm so clever but

155

I'm not. The police should have locked me up and thrown away the key a long time ago. I'm a menace. I used to go into stores and knock over breakable stuff on purpose. I jump into the streets just to see if I can cause car crashes. Believe me, not even the police could punish me any more than I'm punishing myself at this very moment. The worst thing is, they'd probably blame your mom.'

That was probably true. 'Well, we aren't calling the police. Carter Junior is fine and you are too, and everything is back to normal.' I reached across the couch and touched her hand.

'Joey, I've made a decision,' she announced. 'I'm going back to school.'

'Don't go yet,' I pleaded.

'I got what I came for,' she said. 'Carter Junior is back and I promised myself I'd be a more hopeful person if he was found – and less angry.'

'Don't go,' I said forlornly. 'You are my only friend and I'll never meet another girl I love so much.'

'You won't have to,' she said, and squeezed my hand. 'But my suspension is up and your mother is coming home, so it's time to leave.'

'Then just give me one more day,' I begged. 'Just one.'

'Why?' she asked.

'I can't tell you,' I replied, 'but let me do what I have to do and you can have one more day with Carter Junior.'

'Till tomorrow night,' she agreed. 'Only because I prefer to hitchhike in the dark.'

'In the dark?' I remarked. 'That is dangerous.'

'That's what you love about me,' she said, and raised her blind-girl stick up above her head. 'I'm dangerous – and you never know when I'll *strike*!'

I liked that because I was naturally jumpy.

14

THE SCREAM

When I woke up I had no idea that so much of Dad was inside me. Maybe putting that key in my mouth had unlocked all the hidden little parts of me that were just like him and I was his key as much as he was mine, and somehow we were locked together. All I knew for sure was that I had to return to his apartment if we were ever going to unlock everything bad between us.

When I left Olivia and Carter Junior, I quietly locked the door behind me and ran through the cool morning air across town to

Alley O and his old door. I knew he might have a new key and be inside but I had to take that chance because of what I was desperate to do. Before I unlocked his door I flipped open his mail slot and sniffed the stale air that drifted out. It didn't smell of coffee. Maybe he was still asleep, or maybe not. I stuck my key in the lock and slowly gave it a turn. It clicked open and the door chirped towards me.

'Dad?' I said quietly.

There was no reply, and I was relieved, because once I closed his door behind me I marched directly to the crib and climbed in and curled up under the blue blanket with my head on the special pillow faster than I could ask myself why I was acting like the baby when I should be acting like the man. Someday I was going to be a man and Carter Junior was going to be a boy, and I didn't want my dad to still be a baby. I wanted him to be my father. That's what I was thinking as I slipped my thumb into my mouth for the last time because I knew when I woke up I was going to have to be a man.

But I woke up screaming like a baby. It wasn't all my screaming. Dad was screaming too. His face was twisted up in horror and pressed against the bars of the crib as if he was a trapped prisoner in a terrifying prison. When I saw him I started screaming louder, and leaped up onto my feet and wobbled around on the mattress like I was standing up in a canoe and about to flip over. Then he stepped back and staggered for a moment before he wilted straight down like a stack of paper cut-outs of himself. His body just seemed to fold up into a neat pile of clothes, like everything else perfectly placed in his apartment – except for his leathery face. When he finally turned towards me his expression was a wordless mask of pain, and that's when I could see he was more afraid of me than I was of him.

'Dad,' I finally said. 'Are you OK?' And the moment I said his name I could feel something shift in my heart, something as tiny as a little gear in a watch, and I knew that gear would turn a slightly larger gear, which would turn an even larger gear until bigger and more power-ful gears began to turn the special gift in my heart, and I knew I better hang onto the crib railing because suddenly I could feel what he was feeling, and when it hit me I had to grab the bars of the crib to steady myself and bite down on my lip to keep from crying.

He lifted his head and peeked out at me with one eye like a dog that had been bad and beaten.

'Dad,' I said softly. 'Are you OK?'

'I heard you the first time,' he replied coldly. His lips were peeled back as if his mouth had been carved out with a can opener. He sat up a bit more. 'Now tell me, what are you doing in my house?'

'You can't steal Carter Junior and keep him here,' I said. 'If you want the baby you have to come home. That's what I'm here to tell you.'

He seemed to think about that as he unfolded himself and stood. 'He'd be fine with me here,' he replied. 'I'm a new man. I'm not the old bad dad I was. I've hit bottom and bounced back up and am better for it.'

'Well, it looks like you hit bottom face-first,' I replied, reaching out to touch the wormy-red scars where seams of patchwork skin over-lapped.

He stepped back and looked away from me. 'My face is still healing,' he said, sounding wounded as he scratched at a flap of skin by his ear. 'It will smooth over, given time.'

'It doesn't look so good,' I remarked. 'You should go to the hospital.'

'I already have,' he replied. 'I got some medicine, and while there I even tried to see your mom and tell her I was getting better, but she took one look at me and pitched a fit.'

'Can you blame her? Take a look in the mirror,' I suggested, and pointed to a small table mirror on his chest of drawers. 'You won't see the face of a man who looks like he is getting better.'

'The face doesn't tell the whole story,' he said.

'Then what does?' I asked. 'What could possibly tell me something different than what I already know about you? What?'

'Well, do you know that old Frankenstein movie?' he asked. 'With Boris Karloff playing the monster?'

'I know it,' I said.

'Well, remember the part,' he said, 'where the monster goes into the forest and finds the blind man – and they drink wine and smoke a cigar and then the blind man says, "Before you came I was all alone. It is bad to be alone."'

I cut in. 'And Frankenstein replies, "Alone – bad. Friend – good,"' I said, remembering it well because Olivia used to play the blind man and I would have to play the monster. She liked the way I could imitate his voice.

'And then,' Dad said enthusiastically with the blood rising through the canals of his face like the climbing red lines of a thermometer. 'And then,' he repeated, 'the blind man and Frankenstein shake hands in friendship. And if *they* can shake hands then *we* can shake hands.' He reached out to shake mine.

I looked at his hand as if it was on fire.

'Friend?' he said hopefully.

'Remember what the blind man says,' I reminded him. '"There is *good* and there is *bad*," and Frankenstein repeats, "There *is* good and there *is* bad." And he says it like he *means* it – like he knows there is a difference.'

'I know the difference,' Dad said.

'Then act like it,' I shot back a little too sharply, which made me feel bad because I've had my own thousand and one troubles, and other people put up with me even when I knew the difference between good and bad and right and wrong but couldn't act the right way.

'It upsets me that your mother won't let me have Carter Junior,' he said, getting back to that.

'Because you scare us,' I replied.

'It's just my face that's scary,' he countered.

'It's not just your face that's the problem – it's what's under the skin,' I said.

'Don't think I haven't looked in the mirror,' he said, squinting unevenly. 'I have. Believe me, I've had to look past my face for something deeper inside me that was better – something I did that was good – and that something good is Carter Junior.' He turned and pointed towards the baby photo of Carter Junior on his desk. 'He's named after me,' he said firmly. 'He's my second chance. My job is not to screw him up.'

'You mean like you did to me?'

'You know, Joey,' Dad said, 'you might not like what I'm about to say but maybe you aren't as screwed up as you think you are. Maybe when you look in the mirror you should look a little deeper and see what is good about yourself. Maybe you are hurting yourself by walking around thinking that everyone thinks you are a mess.'

'Mom doesn't think I'm a mess,' I said. 'She thinks I'm the man of the house.'

'And I suppose that being a mess in the hospital makes her the woman of the house?' he asked, sneering a bit as he nervously picked at the pleats of skin on his face as if he was removing the bits of crust on a sandwich.

'She's getting better on the inside,' I said. 'And when she comes home she will be the boss.'

He pulled off a strip of dead skin.

'Don't pick at your face like that,' I cautioned. 'You'll only make it worse.'

'Nothing could make it worse,' he replied, and balled the skin up between his fingertip and thumb. 'Except for one thing – everyone can see how much I've changed for the worse on the outside, but no one can see how much I've changed for the better on the inside.'

'Then stop trying to steal the baby,' I repeated.

'But we'd be happy here together in this place,' he said, and waved his arm around to show it off. 'I have it all set up for him and he'd slowly get used to me, and see the good in me.'

'No. That is not going to happen. If you want to be with Carter Junior, then being home is the best place for you,' I said. 'You might look like a monster, but if you don't behave like one then your family won't care what you look like.'

'But when I came to the house he was afraid of me and he screamed,' he said sadly.

'He didn't scream at your face. He only screamed because you grabbed him and ran down the street,' I replied. 'But if you showed up and were nice then he'd just think you were nice.'

'What about you?' he asked. 'Don't I scare you?'

'Yeah, but I came to find you anyway,' I said. 'I'd rather have you at home than have you creeping up on us all the time.'

'What about your mom?' he asked. 'She hates me.'

'Yep,' I said. 'She sure does. But she knows what it's like to try to get better for the family. So if you are trying to get better then I think she'll give you another chance.'

'But she really hates me,' he repeated. 'Deeply.'

'Don't be a coward,' I replied. 'She deserves to hate you even more. Just say you are sorry and mean it.'

He stood motionless as he thought about something while the pink scars on his neck stretched and closed like a fish breathing through gills. 'But what if I just want the baby and my own fresh start?' he said. 'What if that is all the family I want?'

'That's up to you,' I replied, and climbed out of the crib. He looked at me like he wanted to rush forward and hug me or wrestle me to the ground. I couldn't tell what he wanted to do and I didn't think he could either, so I side-stepped around him and headed towards the hallway. Then before he could say anything more I turned and lobbed the key onto his bed.

'I won't be back here,' I said, and I meant it. 'But you know where we live. Right now I'm the man of the house and my rule number one for you is, *No family, then no baby*. It's up to you.' After that I walked out the door.

15

HOUSE-OF-PIGZA

I slapped on a fresh patch like I was snapping a seatbelt round my middle. I had bathed and fed Carter Junior and put him to sleep upstairs in his doughnut doggy bed, and then I tiptoed downstairs and carried a chair into the middle of the living room and stared at the inside of the front door like it was a movie that hadn't yet started. It had been a crazy day so far and it wasn't over with yet, because once the sun goes down around here it seems like all the action starts up.

But when I ran back from Dad's this

morning, with the sun high in the sky and a flock of birds chirping in the back yard, the telephone had rung. I looked out the kitchen window, where Olivia was wearing a pair of my jeans and a T-shirt, and Carter Junior was wrapped in a blanket and wearing a hat as they played the game Olivia now called 'human birdfeeder'. She had sprinkled breadcrumbs all over their clothes, and about a hundred birds seemed to be sitting on them. They were smiling. I was smiling, and I picked up the phone and then I was grinning.

'Joey?' Mom said excitedly.

'That's my name!' I said like a cartoon woodpecker. 'Don't wear it out.'

'You sound full of life,' she said brightly in her old playful Mom voice, and instantly my special gift nearly floated me off the floor as my lungs filled with the hot air of happiness.

'You sound super extra-great,' I said.

'I am,' she said. 'I feel like an old banger that went into the shop and I'm coming out all snazzed up.'

'Snazzy!' I repeated because I love words with extra 'zz's in them. 'That sounds pawzzz-i-tive.'

She laughed. 'How's Carter Junior?' she asked.

'Perfectly Pigza! Bigger and better and look-ing for you,' I said. 'He's talking now, and eating steaks and smoking cigars, and he wants his sweetheart mom!'

'Hmmmm,' she hummed, like she could taste him. 'Can't wait to kiss his belly.'

'I'll give him a bath,' I said. 'So he doesn't taste like one of the dogs.'

'Is Olivia still there?' she asked. 'It was so nice of her to visit me.'

'Yes,' I said, 'but I'm bummed out because she's going back to school.'

'You'll be doing the same,' she said, remind-ing me. 'So give her a kiss goodbye for me.'

'Will do!' I said snappily, and smiled because now I had a reason to kiss her.

'Have you seen your dad around?' she finally asked.

I knew that was coming. 'Yeah,' I said.

'Oh,' she replied coldly, and her voice changed so quickly that right away I felt like someone had poked a hole in my lungs.

'Did he try to steal the baby?' she asked.

'He borrowed him for a moment,' I said quickly, 'but I got him right back. It was like a tiny visit between them,' I added so she wouldn't get worked up.

'Oh,' she said again, and went silent. I didn't think silence was a good place for her, so before she could get all knotted up about Dad I blurted out in my happy voice, 'So when are you coming home so I can bake you a cake?'

'Tonight,' she gushed. 'I'll be home for dinner. I'm packing up my stuff and I'll see my therapist, and after that I'm dropping by the hair salon to get my nails done and a pedicure, and I'm coming home all dolled up to see my boys.'

'We'll be here waiting,' I replied, with a big smile on the inside. She sounded just like my old mom because when she had a manicure and a pedicure it was like she also had a mental-cure.

'Love you and see you soon,' she said, and the moment the receiver went down I was in a hyper-panic.

'Olivia!' I hollered out the window. 'Have you ever baked a cake? I need a cake for Mom – like a cake the size of a whale.'

'Shush,' she said softly from where she and Carter Junior were together like statues of Saint Francis with birds eating out of their hands. 'Just call the bakery,' she said in a half-whisper, 'and order one. That's what we do at our house.'

That made sense because I didn't want to mess up the kitchen, so I picked up the phone and ordered Mom a carrot cake, and when the baker asked if I wanted to write something special on the icing I knew exactly what to say. *'Inner strength. Self-love. Pigza pride. You have it!'*

'How about just saying, *You are the number-one mom in the world?*' the baker asked.

'Nah,' I replied. 'She's number one in her own way.'

Hearing from Mom and ordering the cake was a really extra-cheesy, extra-good start to a day that I knew was going to be a rough ride down a long road, and I wasn't sure what would be waiting for me at the end.

In the early evening Olivia and I took Carter Junior and walked quietly down to the bakery and picked up the cake, but it didn't feel like a cake for a celebration because when we got back home Olivia said, 'It's time for me to go.'

I put the cake in the roach-proof refrigerator while Olivia put on her black school dress and folded up her extra panties and shoved them in a pocket. Then she hung her *HELP! Blind Girl Hitchhiking!* sign around her neck. 'I'm ready,' she announced, and stood by the front door. 'Do you want to say goodbye?'

'I'm holding Carter Junior in my arms, so don't hit me with your blind-girl stick,' I said. 'But I just want to say that I really love having you as a girlfriend.'

She raised an eyebrow. 'Are you going to kiss me goodbye?' she asked. 'Because if not, I'm out the door. I can't stand a lingering exit.'

I stepped towards her. She reached out for Carter Junior and I handed him over.

'He's first,' she said, and gave him so many kisses that I was jealous. When she gave him back to me I thought she had used all her kisses up. But she had one more.

'You're next,' she said.

I held Carter Junior on my hip and stuck my neck forward. I closed my eyes and we carefully moved closer like two real blind people kissing. It seemed to take so long to reach her face I wondered if I had missed it and might just kiss her on the earlobe as I passed by. But it turned out OK. It was like closing your eyes and slowly pressing your fingertips together. It was a perfect kiss. Then I kissed her again for Mom.

'Take care of Carter Junior,' she said.

'I will,' I promised.

'Be good to your mother,' she said. 'She needs you.'

'I will,' I replied.

'Learn braille and write me,' she said. Then she leaned forward and whispered in my ear, 'Send me secret Pigza love letters that I can keep in a drawer wrapped in black ribbon and sprinkled with rose perfume.'

'Perfumed Pigza?' I yelped, and made an icky face. I really wasn't ready for that. Plus I had another problem. 'I have lousy spelling,' I said.

'Guess what? I have really lousy reading,' she replied. 'Relax. You worry too much.'

Then she turned the lock on the front door and pulled it open.

'Sorry the porch light is out,' I said in a goofy voice.

She smiled, then in an instant she lifted her blind-girl stick and cracked me hard across the shin. 'Don't forget me,' she said.

'Never,' I whimpered. 'I think this one will leave a scar.'

'That's body-braille for love,' she said. 'It should hurt until I return for Christmas.' And then, just as she had arrived, she turned round and *tap-tap-tapped* her way down the steps and *thwack-thwack-thwacked* her way to the corner and took a right and my heart went with her, but since I was the man of the house I had to take care of Carter Junior plus I had a guest arriving, so I went back inside and locked the door and got his dinner ready and bathed him and put him to bed, and then I got the chair and set it in the living room and from that moment I have been staring at the door.

I was worrying about Olivia. I wasn't an oracle. A real oracle actually sees into the future and knows all the details – the good and the bad – of what is about to happen. But nobody can really do that. I couldn't see how her journey would go, but hoping for a happy ending is kind of the next best thing to being an oracle. I closed my eyes and hoped that Olivia made it back to school OK. I hoped it so much that I could see her get into a nice car with a good older person who would drive her directly up to the front door of her school and say to her, 'Good luck with your anger management,' and she'd reply, 'Thank you, kind person, but my boyfriend Joey Pigza helped me get that under control.' Then she would walk into the school and tap her way down a long hallway to her dormitory and crawl into her own bed, and the next morning wake up with hope in her heart and a big black outline of Carter Junior in her head where that black box had tortured her for so long.

I could imagine it all with my eyes closed and it made me feel hopeful. And then the moment I opened my eyes it happened.

'Ding-Dog!'

It was Mr Fong with dinner, I thought, but when I hopped up and opened the door it was not Mr Fong. It was the other delivery guy, my dad, and he had delivered himself. He was standing with a suitcase in one hand and a bag of takeaway food in the other.

'Where is Mr Fong?' I asked.

'We've all eaten enough pizza for a lifetime,' he announced. 'From now on it's Chinese food. It's your mother's favourite.'

I reached out and took the food. 'Come in,' I said.

'The food might be cold,' he warned. 'I've been waiting across the street. It took you long enough to say goodbye to your girlfriend.'

He walked into the kitchen and looked around. 'It's so clean,' he said. 'Nice.'

'And no more filthy roaches,' I pointed out.

'I hate them too,' he agreed.

'We have something in common,' I said.

'We have your mom in common too,' he added nervously, and pressed his fingers against his face as if a piece of it needed sticking back on. 'Is she here?'

'Not yet,' I said. 'Carter Junior is asleep and I'm waiting for her.'

He looked up at the ceiling as if he could see Carter Junior in his doughnut doggy bed. 'How do you think your mom will act when she sees me?' he asked.

'Well, when I'm hopeful about it I see her coming into the house and seeing you and not splitting your head open with a meat cleaver, or mine for letting you in, and then she'll run upstairs and check on the baby, and when she sees that he is OK she'll take a deep breath and count to ten, and then she'll come downstairs and I'll kiss her a lot while she kisses me a lot and tells me I did such a good job and was her man of the house and that I was her anchor while she got better, and then she'll spot you hovering in a corner looking pretty pathetic and right at that moment it will be time for me to go to my room, and quite honestly, the rest is up to you two. I'm not an oracle. I'm just a hopeful boy. I can imagine how everything turns out really well, but it will be up to you and Mom to make it happen.'

'That's kind of what I'm hoping for,' he remarked. 'Do you see anything else?'

'Just that I'm wired because you are wired because your mom was wired,' I said. 'So it figures that I love Carter Junior because Mom loves Carter Junior, and if you love Carter Junior then we'll all love you too.'

He nodded. 'That's real good,' he said eagerly. 'Can I tell her that?'

'No. Or yes. But whatever you tell her it better come from the heart and you better live up to it, because even though you are here I'm still the man of the house. You got that?'

'Yes,' he mumbled.

'Now go set the table,' I ordered. 'If she comes home it would be a really good start to have dinner like a family.'

While he got the plates and knives and forks and napkins I got the cake out of the refrigerator and onto a platter and set it down right on top of Mom's plate like she could just drop her face into it and eat the whole thing. I thought all that sugar would put her in the right mood.

Then Dad and I sat down, but we didn't

serve the Chinese food or talk to each other. We were like little plastic family-member statues just staring at the door and waiting for the unknown to happen.

Then I heard it in the distance, *tap-tap-tap*. It turned the corner and was coming up our street. Then it got closer and louder. And then it was in front of our house. *Tap-tap* . . . and then there was a little scream.

It couldn't have been Olivia returning because she always made everyone else scream. I jumped up, and in an instant ran out onto the front porch. The light from the open door shone down the steps. Mom was at the bottom with a shopping bag in one hand and her purse in the other. She was standing unevenly with all her weight on one high heel because the other one had snapped.

'Welcome back to the House-of-Pigza,' I cried out, and threw my arms up into the air like I was a human firecracker going off.

'Dang shoe,' she said. 'What an entrance!'

She kicked off her other shoe and ran up the stairs and gave me a big hug just as I had imagined it. Then she kissed me all over. Then she said I was her anchor and her man of the house like I knew she would.

And then the other man finally got up some courage and stuck his head round the door-jamb.

'Hi, Fran,' he said, sheepishly. 'Welcome home.'

She just stood there shaking her head. 'I knew it,' she said dryly. 'I could see it clear as day in my mind as I was walking up the street. I said to myself, *Fran, be prepared because that crazy, no-good husband is going to be in your house looking for a second chance for the hundredth time.*'

Wow! She really *was* an oracle!

'Well, you always had good vision,' he replied with as much of a smile as he could manage on his messed-up face. 'Now come on in,' he said. 'Someone baked you a cake.'

The first thing she did was go upstairs and get Carter Junior, and even though he was sleepy she brought him down and I could see where her lipstick was all over his little beaming face.

Then she saw her cake and took a moment to read it, then turned to me with tears in her eyes. I was grinning like a lunatic and hopping up and down along with the dogs. 'We're two of a kind,' she said.

'Double that,' Dad added in, and pointed towards Carter Junior, then poked himself in the chest. 'House rules are that four of a kind beats a pair of Pigzas every day of the week.'

Mom looked over at him. I could read her mind. She was going to make some crack about *face* cards. But then she thought better of it. Instead, she said, 'Well, welcome back, stranger. You better be playing with a full deck.'

I stood there watching them and thinking that I should say something about all we had gone through in the past and our great future together, but then there are times when saying nothing is like being the most all-seeing oracle in the world.

'I'm going to my room for a while,' I announced. 'It's been a long week.'

I kissed Mom, then gave Dad a hug and didn't look back as I closed my bedroom door and kicked off my shoes. Maybe it's a little bit of a spook house, having Mom and Dad back and a big photo of my wired granny smoking a cigarette on the wall over my bed, but it's my house and they are my dark shadows and bright panes of light and under every roof there is a wacky family and this is mine and I love them. I think I'm finally going to have a good day. So don't be a stranger. Stop on by. There is always an extra slice waiting for you at the House-of-Pigza.

JOEY PIGZA
SWALLOWED THE KEY

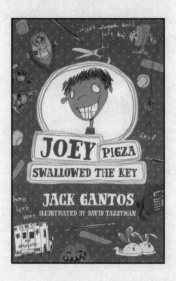

Joey is a good kid, maybe even a great kid,
but his teachers say he's WIRED . . . they
never know what he's going to do next.

He can't sit still for more than a
minute . . . Joey is BUZZING!

978 0 440 87071 5

JOEY PIGZA LOSES CONTROL

If people think Joey Pigza has problems,
they should meet his dad! When Joey gets to
spend the summer with him, he soon finds
out why Mom was so worried . . .

Can Joey live life his dad's way –
or will the chaos take over?

978 0 440 87053 1

WHAT WOULD
JOEY PIGZA DO?

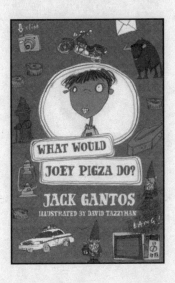

Grandma wants Joey to find a friend, stop
running around after his nutty parents, and
start looking after himself. But Joey's got
other plans – he's going to be Mr Helpful.

Can Joey the superhero succeed in his
mission to keep everybody smiling?

978 0 440 87054 8

I AM NOT
JOEY PIGZA

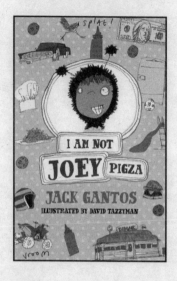

Joey's long-lost dad is back after hitting
the lottery jackpot. He wants them to start
a whole new life by opening a diner and
changing their name from Pigza to Heinz!

They can change Joey's name, but can
they change the boy inside?

978 0 440 87055 5